The Mercenary's Bride

The Brides of Inverfyre #1

CLAIRE DELACROIX

Books by Claire Delacroix

MEDIEVAL ROMANCE

The Bride Quest:
The Princess
The Damsel
The Heiress
The Countess
The Beauty
The Temptress

The Rogues of Ravensmuir:
The Rogue
The Scoundrel
The Warrior

The Jewels of Kinfairlie:
The Beauty Bride
The Rose Red Bride
The Snow White Bride
The Ballad of Rosamunde

The True Love Brides:
The Renegade's Heart
The Highlander's Curse
The Frost Maiden's Kiss
The Warrior's Prize

The Brides of Inverfyre:
The Mercenary's Bride
The Runaway Bride (coming soon)

Rogues & Angels:
One Knight Enchanted

For information about Deborah Cooke contemporary
romances and paranormal romances, please visit:

HTTP://DEBORAHCOOKE.COM

PROLOGUE

he air simmered.

The sun was hot enough to burn, even early in the season, and Quentin was so parched that he could not recall the feel of water in his mouth. All the same, he did not rise from the road. He remained where he had been abandoned—beaten, robbed, and bleeding— and watched the carrion birds circle overhead. They were dark against the brilliant blue of the sky. The road was empty in either direction. There was no sound but the wind and the calls of the birds that soon would make a meal of him.

He did not know how many of his bones were broken or how much blood he had shed. Both counts must have been considerable, given how shattered he felt and how many assailants had

1

attacked him. Whether his right eye was merely swollen or more damaged than that, he did not know. His magnificent destrier was gone, along with its trap, his armor, his sword, his money, his food, his water. He literally had the shirt on his back and no more.

He had lost everything, but worse, he had no hope. Quentin did not have it within him to fight any longer. Who would care if he died?

He would never return to England, much less Scotland.

He would never reach Seville.

He would never prove himself to the Hawk of Inverfyre. Anger rose within him at the memory of their final exchange and fury kindled within Quentin. What was his crime? He had loved the Hawk's daughter, Mhairi, loved her for her ferocity and passion—and her determination to learn the arts of war. He had tutored her, openly at first and then in secret, believing his liege lord was wrong to keep his daughter from the knowledge she yearned to possess.

In truth, Quentin could not deny Mhairi. He would do any deed for her. He had ridden south and spent seven years as a mercenary, earning a fortune so that he could return and request the honor of her hand in marriage.

He rolled to his back and scowled at the birds. It was all lost, and his hope was replaced with anger. He would not even be in Spain without the Hawk's challenge. He would not be injured. He would not be without the means to earn his way ever again.

He would not have lost Mhairi forever.

The birds cried to their fellows as they dipped lower but Quentin gritted his teeth. He was not dead yet, and as God was his witness, he would see Mhairi one last time.

He had made her a promise that was yet unfulfilled.

And he would have his vengeance upon the Hawk, if it was the last deed he did.

CHAPTER ONE

Inverfyre, Scotland—December 1432

hairi passed through Inverfyre village alongside her mother, the two women riding to hunt together. Mhairi carried her peregrine on her fist while her mother carried the gyrfalcon she had favored for hunting these past few years. Both women were dressed simply, with high boots and slit kirtles that allowed them greater movement. Both had braided their hair and would abandon their veils and circlets as soon as they left the village behind. Both had crossbows slung from their saddles and daggers in their belts. They wore leather jerkins and heavy gloves with long cuffs.

Their horses stepped high in anticipation of a run and perhaps because of the crisp snap of winter in the air. The hour was so early that the mist was still rising from the river and the day promised to be fine. Beaters ran ahead of them and dogs behind, and a trio of men followed to aid in bringing the kill back to the hall. They had jested about bringing a wagon, for these forays of Aileen and Mhairi were known to fill the larder. There would be a feast the night before First Advent, which was only days away.

Mhairi's peregrine, Freya, was restless on her fist, perhaps feeling some of Mhairi's own anticipation. The jesses bound the bird's ankles there and she was yet hooded, but at the very least, Freya anticipated that she would soon be set free to do what she did best.

Mhairi loved to hunt almost as much as Freya. She and her mother were so similar in their thinking and strategy that they spoke little on such forays, yet worked in perfect harmony. It was a relief to be away from the expectations of others, even for part of a day, and Mhairi also liked to make a tangible contribution to Inverfyre and its occupants. All would eat well after she and her mother returned home.

The Hawk, her father, often joined them, but on this day, he was occupied with his ledgers. Mhairi knew he would have preferred to abandon them in favor of the hunt. It was only after enduring the stern reminder of his steward with regard to the taxes owed to the king at the end of the month that he had surrendered the battle and agreed to remain at the hall. Her older brother, Nigel, had been compelled to remain with the Hawk to learn yet more about the administration of Inverfyre. Henry, the castellan, would also witness the balancing of the ledgers. Nigel was a good hunter, but as oldest son, had more responsibilities than that.

One blessing was that Evangeline would not be accompanying them. Mhairi's older sister could not be silent, even in a forest, and certainly not while game was being stalked. If Evangeline had joined them, she would have torn a hem, broken a nail, chattered endlessly and they would have returned with significantly less for the larder. Better she lounged in the hall, pretending to embroider but truly reviewing the names of her admirers.

When word passed through the village of their venture, more villagers came out to watch them ride past. Mhairi was always astounded by how quickly tidings could pass from one house to the next. She rode to the left and slightly behind her mother, letting Aileen proceed first as Lady of Inverfyre.

"Bring us a hart, my lady!" shouted the smith. "Time it is for venison stew, to my thinking."

Aileen laughed. "To mine, as well," she replied. "We shall see what crosses our path this day."

"A good hunt to you," called the miller's wife. "I say take the hares. There are too many of them in my garden, to be sure."

"Perhaps we will set some traps," Aileen called and Mhairi smiled. She knew her mother hoped to take at least one deer. This time of year, the cook liked to salt some meat for the months ahead, in case stores were not abundant or the weather poor.

Mhairi watched her mother, admiring her combination of resolve and grace. She waved and smiled, confident and so very kind. Mhairi's chest tightened as she thought of the love between her mother and father, and she hoped ardently that she, too, could find such love.

Although with Quentin banished from her life forever, it seemed unlikely.

He had probably forgotten her, a young girl enamored of the arts of war. He had probably dismissed her interest as whimsy or a phase. He had probably found another post with a baron or a duke, and had married well. It had been seven years, and though Mhairi recalled every detail about her father's former Captain of the Guard, she doubted that Quentin recalled her at all.

Or perhaps he thought of her with the affection a man might reserve for a young cousin.

If he had been haunted by the memory of her, surely he would have returned? There had not been a word from him since her father had cast him from the gates for daring to defy his command.

They passed through the gates, followed by the villagers. Aileen's gyrfalcon, Skuld, flapped and cried, agitated by some movement or other. Mhairi saw her mother murmur to the bird as a boy training with the falconer reached to take her. No sooner had he gripped Skuld's jesses and the bird loosed her talons from Aileen's glove than a man in

7

a heavy wool cloak broke out of the crowd. He hurled himself at the Lady of Inverfyre before any could stop him.

"My lady!" he roared, even as Aileen was shoved from the saddle beneath his weight.

Guards shouted. Villagers gasped. The hunting birds screamed and flapped. Mhairi cried out as her mother fell to the ground. But before anyone could, an arrow sliced through the air. It had been aimed at Aileen, and missed her only because she was no longer in her saddle.

It buried itself in the wall of the opposite hut, quivering there.

Mhairi spun to look for the archer while all the others crowded around her mother. A man with a long bow stood just outside the village walls, smirking. He had a tangle of ginger hair and watched with undisguised pleasure as Aileen fell.

He raised a fist. "Justice for the MacLarens!" he cried. "The line of Magnus Armstrong must die!"

Mhairi had dropped the reins as soon as she saw the arrow.

"My lady!" said the falconer's boy, right by Mhairi's side. He clearly anticipated her reaction for he raised his fist to take Freya.

By the time the rebel cried out, she had already loaded a bolt. She fired her crossbow while he was in the midst of his cry. She moved quickly and decisively, just as Quentin had taught her. The bolt nicked the man's shoulder just as the last word crossed his lips and sent him spinning backward. He swore with vigor, dropping his own bow and clapping his hand to his injured shoulder. Mhairi saw the blood flowing between his fingers.

She muttered a curse beneath her breath that her aim had been off. She had hoped to strike him in the throat. She loaded another bolt, but he ducked into the forest.

"You!" he shouted at her. "You and all your kin will be slaughtered!"

He might have said more, but two villagers with scythes headed in pursuit. He took one look at them, snatched his bow, then fled like a rabbit into the undergrowth of the surrounding forest. Hooting and laughter was heard from the woods.

"The MacLarens," Reinhard said and spat at the ground in disgust. He was an old comrade of her father's and had been made Captain of the Guard after Quentin's departure. "They are the ones who should be hunted to the ground and slaughtered. They could not keep a holding, but neither can they abandon the pursuit of it." He nodded at Mhairi. "A fine shot, my lady."

"Thank you, Reinhard, but I wanted to kill him."

"It might be better that you did not," the older man said with a frown. "He grows bolder, which is worrisome."

Mhairi turned to her mother, who sat on the ground surrounded by villagers and servants. Mhairi dismounted quickly, noting that guards had seized the man who had pushed Aileen from her saddle.

Aileen's white gyrfalcon was held by the boy still

9

and flapping wildly. Guinevere, the healer, pushed her way through the ranks of villagers, her expression grim, and her son Talbot followed her. He murmured to Skuld, taking the peregrine from the other boy's glove gently. He had brought a piece of raw meat and the bird almost snatched it from his hand in her flustered state. The feathers on her hood shook with her agitation, no doubt exacerbated by her inability to see. The bird calmed quickly beneath Talbot's care and it was not the first time that Mhairi thought the boy understood the language of predatory birds.

Freya smelled the meat and began to cry for a piece of her own, even as Mhairi crouched at her mother's side. "Are you injured?" she asked, but her mother shook her head.

"Startled. Perhaps bruised." Aileen smiled. "But it would have been infinitely worse without that man's intervention." She pointed to the stranger restrained by the guards.

"But my lady, he assaulted you," protested Reinhard.

"He did as much to save me," Aileen countered. "Mhairi, you must have followed the trajectory of the arrow."

"It would have gone through your throat, *Maman*," Mhairi confessed and a ripple of shock passed through the gathered company.

"And a bruise, no matter how black, is better than that," Aileen concluded, accepting Guinevere's inspection of her wrist. Aileen had put her hand out

to brace herself against the fall and a bruise was already rising there. There was a bustle from the keep and Mhairi knew without a glance that her father was charging toward them.

"Help me to my feet," her mother said with quiet heat. "If he finds me like this, I will not be able to leave my chamber before spring."

"If then, my lady," Reinhard said.

There was a chuckle of acknowledgement at the truth in their words, and Aileen was standing by her horse by the time the Hawk arrived. His gaze was avid and his lips tight as he heard the tale from a dozen sources. He glanced several times to Mhairi to verify that he was being told the truth, and she nodded that he was.

"And you made a fine shot in retaliation," the Hawk said to Mhairi, pride in his voice at her achievement.

She could not help but bristle, for he had not always thought well of her skills.

"I had a good teacher," she said with a measure of defiance, knowing that her father would not be pleased by the reminder. He caught his breath, then he pivoted to the cloaked man who had unhorsed Aileen and was still being held captive.

Mhairi was certain that her father had not abandoned the point, but that he would pursue it in private.

She would wait.

"And who are you?" the Hawk demanded of the man. "And how is it that you guessed the intent of

11

the MacLarens beyond the walls? Are you one of them?"

"Not I," the man said and something about his voice caught Mhairi's ear. It was deep and resonant, and his words were slow. It seemed familiar, but she was certain it could not be. Then he cast back his hood and her heart stopped. "As for who I might be, I understand that I have been a good teacher."

His face was marred and he wore a patch over his right eye, but it was Quentin de Montgomerie as surely as it was December at Inverfyre.

And he was looking at her, with something that might have been admiration.

Mhairi could not utter a sound.

Indeed, her heart had stopped.

Quentin!

"'Twas a fine shot," he acknowledged, then shook off the grip of those who had been holding him. "The angle was less than ideal, yet your speed did not diminish your accuracy. You let your instincts guide your bolt, which is best." He gave a little bow, grimacing as if it pained him. "I am most impressed."

At the Hawk's nod, the guards released Quentin and he fumbled for a walking stick. It was only when he had it and straightened, that Mhairi saw the rest of the change. He limped now and was bent instead of tall and straight. He had lost weight, for his face was gaunt. He was less powerful as well, for the vigor with which he gripped the head of the walking stick showed his reliance upon it. He was garbed more simply than once he had been and more poorly. His cloak was rough dark wool and his boots looked to be nigh worn through. He was dirty from the road, as the knight she had known would never have tolerated, but he had no belongings so she knew he had no choice.

Quentin's fine armor and trappings were as gone as his good looks, as evidently was his horse. He was still taller than her, still a man who steadily met her gaze. Quentin had never been one to flirt or tease—he listened, he considered, and he acted with resolve. When he laughed, it was with merriment, not at the expense of another. Mhairi had always admired those traits but she saw a new anger simmering in his eyes. It startled her for he had always been temperate and loyal, and she wondered how long it had been since he had laughed.

She wanted to console him.

His sleeve covered his right hand where he gripped the walking stick. He pulled a knife from his belt as he approached her, offering it on the palm of his left hand before the Hawk could step forward to intervene. He granted her father a quelling glance, as if daring the Hawk to stop him, then presented the dagger to Mhairi. He leaned heavily on the walking stick as he bowed again before her and she was shaken by the change in him.

He looked like an old man, not a warrior who had been gone a mere seven years. He could not have seen thirty summers, for the age between them had not been so great as that. Clearly, his injuries were severe.

"I made a promise to a lady," Quentin said, his voice a wondrous low rumble that still made Mhairi shiver. It was easy to recall his murmur in her ear as he corrected her stance, all those years before and how she had thrilled at his fleeting touch—never mind how she had dreamed of him. "And having come precariously close to death, I thought it time to see that pledge kept."

Mhairi knew the sole promise he had made to her, knew it as well as her own name.

A blade of her own, of fine Toledo steel.

That was what he had promised.

And that was what he offered.

But it was his own blade. She recognized it, just as she had recognized him.

Mhairi had to lick her lips twice before she could respond. The gathered group were completely silent, and she was aware of her mother's hand on the Hawk's arm, keeping him from intervening.

It was impossible to forget that she had learned to throw a knife with this very weapon.

Impossible to forget that the lesson in question had seen Quentin expelled from Inverfyre.

It was also impossible to not admire that he had defied her father's edict and returned, just to give this blade to her.

"Not your dagger," she managed to say. "I thought you meant another."

"It is the only blade of Toledo steel in my possession," Quentin said mildly. "It had been my

plan to acquire another, but I am unlikely to find the means now." He shrugged, a casual gesture that did not seem casual at all when his eyes blazed such a vivid hue of green. "Indeed, I have no need of it, not any longer."

Mhairi frowned, for a fighting man always had need of his weapons. Her gaze roved over his humble garb, seeing its import only now. He fought no longer.

But why?

"Why..." she started to ask, then recalled that Quentin had always favored his right hand. He could fight with either hand, all knights of merit could, but his natural preference was for his right.

And that hand remained hidden by the hem of his sleeve.

"What has happened to you?" she demanded, hearing her mother's quick inhalation of disapproval for such boldness, but did not care.

"Take the blade," Quentin said, steel in his tone.

"Show me," Mhairi replied, equally resolute. When he did not move, she reached for his sleeve.

Quentin froze, then he nodded. "I would not show most ladies, but you were always different, Lady Mhairi." His voice softened. "You were always a warrior in your heart and unafraid to face the truth." He extended his left hand and gave her an intent look. She accepted the knife from him, its weight cold in her grasp, knowing that he would not show her otherwise.

Then Quentin flung back his cloak, putting his

right hand atop his left on the head of the walking stick, so that its injury could not be disguised.

The index finger had been carved away and there was a cruel scar upon the back of his hand. The Hawk swore under his breath at the sight and her mother murmured Quentin's name.

"You cannot fight," Mhairi said around the lump in her throat.

"Not well enough to do it long." Quentin's smile was crooked now and more bitter than once it had been. His voice was hard. "I will beg for the rest of my life, unless the Hawk means to keep his pledge to see me executed if I dared return to Inverfyre." He did not so much as glance at the Hawk, his gaze unswerving from Mhairi. She knew her eyes widened, for she had been unaware of this detail. "But I would not have you think I broke my oath to you by choice."

He had returned to Inverfyre, for her, even knowing that it might be his last deed. Mhairi's heart clenched. Heat simmered between them, heat that was both familiar and new. Mhairi hated the anger she sensed within Quentin, though still she was drawn to him. Nay, she was *more* drawn to him than before, and wished she could dismiss his newfound bitterness.

She wished he could be as he had been before.

He suddenly averted his gaze from hers, perhaps glimpsing her thoughts as readily as he had once before. He turned to the Hawk with challenge in his expression.

What would her father do?

Mhairi's heart thundered.

"I trust you do not mean to condemn me for touching your lady wife, as well," Quentin said, his tone colder than the most frigid winter night.

"Of course not," the Hawk said, though his manner was stiff. "I owe you my gratitude, Quentin de Montgomerie, and welcome you to Inverfyre. Will you come to the hall and be my guest this night?"

"Guest?" Quentin echoed. "Do you feed condemned men before their execution at Inverfyre now?" Something in his manner made Mhairi wonder if execution had been his hope, if he had imagined the Hawk might end his misery.

Her father paused, then uttered the question in Mhairi's heart. "Did you mean to provoke me to keep my pledge?"

"I did think you might render the final blow, for you are a man who keeps his word. I ask again: do you mean to treat me as a guest this night and a villain on the morrow?"

"Surely you would not welcome death," Aileen said, clearly trying to diffuse the tension between the two warriors. "Surely you did not court it by your return."

"Surely, I cannot welcome my survival in such a state as this," Quentin replied, his tone harsh. "I have kept the one promise that was outstanding, though, and so my task in this world may be done." He lifted his chin, proud again. "Perhaps I will die this night in your hall, Hawk, and your honor will be served."

"Nay," Mhairi said without meaning to do as much.

Her father cast her an unexpected smile. "Nay, as Mhairi says." He offered his hand to Quentin. "I thank you for your intervention this day, Quentin, for otherwise this moment would be much less merry. I believe it negates the old matter between us. Shall we be allies once more?"

The newly arrived knight hesitated for only a moment, then he put his marred hand into that of the Hawk. The Hawk did not flinch, to Mhairi's pleasure. The two shook hands in agreement and Mhairi could not silence the thrill of excitement in her belly.

Quentin had returned!

The Hawk indicated the keep. "On this night, I bid you come to the hall, eat and drink with me. I would hear of all your adventures these past years."

Quentin was not fooled. The Hawk wished to learn what else he had learned of the MacLarens and their schemes.

"You know Reinhard, of course, who is now Captain of the Guard."

Quentin and Reinhard acknowledged each other, Reinhard's suspicion more than clear. The trio continued toward the keep, her father discussing accommodations for Quentin for that night and doubtless telling him of changes at Inverfyre.

When Mhairi might have followed closely to

hear what was said, her mother claimed Mhairi's hand and held her back.

"What a tribute for a man to risk his life to keep a promise to you," Aileen said quietly. "And it is a fine blade. May I see it?"

Mhairi surrendered it to her mother, who studied it before returning it to her. "I should not take it, for it is his only blade."

"Do not insult him, Mhairi," her mother advised. "Do you find the sight of his scars horrifying?"

"Of course not. Quentin's heart is true, even if he has lost an eye and a finger."

"If not more," Aileen noted with a shrewd glance at her daughter.

"His nature is as it ever was," Mhairi insisted. "He is honorable and keeps his word. Surely that is of greater import than his injuries?"

"Surely it is, if it is true," Aileen replied. "But he is filled with a fury I do not recall."

"Surely it is reasonable that he should feel cheated by his injuries?"

"To feel cheated is one matter," her mother said. "To become bitter and resentful, or worse, to blame another for one's misfortunes, is quite another." She gave Mhairi a hard look. "Though I am saddened to say as much, I will sleep better when Quentin is gone from Inverfyre."

"He saved you!"

"And he has become such a stranger that I wonder why." Aileen shook her head. "He cannot depart soon enough."

Mhairi helped her mother return to the hall, though they did not speak again. She could not help but be saddened by the prospect of Quentin leaving again. It seemed to Mhairi that he had need of some compassion, and where else should he find it but here at Inverfyre, which had been his home.

She had to speak to him as soon as possible, for she doubted she would have many opportunities to do as much. And indeed, she suspected that once he left, he would never return again.

The shy and serious maiden had become a beauty.

Quentin did not know what he had expected, but it had not been Mhairi, grown nigh as tall as him, a slender woman with enticing curves and a familiar resolve in her gaze. He had been shaken by the change in her, and by his own reaction to the sight. He had always found her attractive, but now she shook him to his marrow. He desired her and yearned to speak with her, and wanted her companionship more than ever.

He would be able to deny her nothing at all now, not if she appealed to him, and that made him feel even more vulnerable than he knew he was.

He knew he would savor that first glimpse of her for the rest of his days. She sat astride her palfrey as if born to the saddle, her chin high and the peregrine on her fist. He recalled the tales he had heard over the years of Viking goddesses, beautiful, merciless and forthright. Mhairi's dark blonde hair was bound back in a braid that trailed down her back, that and her simple garb revealing that she was as pragmatic as ever.

But she was an inquisitive child no longer. He doubted she asked others for favors with the same trust and conviction that she had once shown to him. Nay, she had the impassivity of a warrior, or better, a Valkyrie come to claim his soul, and he would have liked to have seen her hunt.

She took after her mother, that was most clear, and perhaps had adopted her cool manner from her peregrine. Her gaze had swept over him as he fumbled to his feet and he wondered if he had imagined a hunter's disdain for the infirm in her blue eyes.

It was clear to Quentin that there could be no place in the world of this fierce maiden for one such as he had become. She would have no tolerance of infirmity of any kind. She would see it as weakness, as a mark that he should be the one culled from her herd, and it was the last indignity that this woman should find him wanting.

What Mhairi did not know was that his injuries were far less than Quentin would have others believe.

He was irked, to be sure, that she of all people did not discern the truth and accepted the view of himself that he presented to others. He had taught her to observe. He had taught her to pierce illusion and that she had not seen past his own disheartened him.

Fury had helped him to drag himself to aid under the hot sun. Anger had fueled his determination to survive and to recover to the best of his abilities. Resentment had driven his footsteps north to Scotland and to Inverfyre, but now the potent emotion he had come to rely upon was changing.

He had been outraged when he had overheard the MacLarens scheming in the forest the night before. He still could not believe the instinctive reaction that had sent him leaping forward to save Lady Aileen. And the sight of Mhairi had shaken him to his marrow—because of the wave of longing it had awakened.

Instead of being executed by the Hawk for daring to defy him again, Quentin was welcomed as a guest. The gesture was the true mark of the Hawk's character, but Quentin felt as if he had lost his lodestone.

He should have been angry with the Hawk still. He should have been resentful that he could not ask for the hand of the woman he desired, now more than ever. But instead, Quentin found himself reconsidering his own choices and finding that his anger lodged there. He had never been worthy of Mhairi, even when whole. No man of sense betrothed his daughter to a man-at-arms in his employ, and the Hawk had good sense. And truly, the Hawk could not be blamed for every choice Quentin had made since leaving Inverfyre so many years before.

It had been his own desire for just a little more coin before returning here that had put Quentin on the road where he had been robbed.

Truly, Inverfyre was as enchanted a holding as he had always heard.

Quentin hobbled to the stables where he had been granted a pallet, struggling to recover the outrage that had been his constant companion since the robbery. Nothing had changed, after all. What would his future be? That of a beggar? It was less, far less, than the life he had hoped to live. It was unjust!

He would yet be whole if he had remained here.

But he had not remained at Inverfyre, because he had provoked his laird with defiance. Quentin had disobeyed the Hawk's command, to be sure, but that man must have seen the truth of his daughter's nature. Mhairi was better with a good tutor than with none at all. She had a skill with a bow and even with a blade that was uncommon. How could a father not encourage a child to follow her desire?

It was a thin argument and he knew it well. His fury ebbed with each step he took through this fair and prosperous holding. Quentin had not blamed the Hawk's protective instinct when he had been initially expelled. He had tried to fulfill the Hawk's challenge and had nigh succeeded. He had been so close to triumph when it all had been snatched away. And now he had no hope of earning such coin again.

For the first time since he had been injured, Quentin felt despair. His anger had nigh deserted him and in its place was only a sense of futility. He felt old and broken, and did not have to exaggerate his limp.

Indeed, he felt the urge to weep for what he had lost, to gnash his teeth at his own part in his misfortune, and knew it was time he found solitude to mourn.

∂ॐ

Mhairi helped her mother to the solar and stood by as Genevieve checked her injuries thoroughly. Her father had retreated to the small chamber where he kept his accounts and her mother refused to see him troubled for what she called a minor incident.

"You will be sore," Genevieve said with a smile when she was done. "But only for a few days. There will be no riding to hunt."

Aileen stretched out on the bed with a wince. "To be sure, none of us will leave Inverfyre until the MacLarens are routed again."

"Why would they attack now?" Mhairi asked.

Her mother shrugged. "Because they are numerous enough. Because one of them is old enough or bold enough or won the support of his kin." She sighed and closed her eyes. "I had thought the matter resolved when so many died in the second assault upon Inverfyre, when your father and I wed, but clearly I was wrong."

"Did Quentin knew of their intent?" Genevieve

24

asked as she packed her bag of herbs. "Or did he simply see them in time?"

"I cannot say," Aileen replied, then yawned. "I have no doubt the Hawk will find the truth and in this moment, I am sufficiently tired to leave the matter in his hands." She smiled at Mhairi. "You do not need to sit with me. Go to Evangeline. Doubtless she is upset by the events of the morning."

"Yes, Maman," Mhairi agreed, having no intention of going to her sister. If she wished to learn what Quentin knew, there was only one sensible person to ask.

But if her plan was guessed, she would be stopped.

The solar occupied the top floor of the tower of Inverfyre, while the chambers of the Hawk's children were on the floor below. The hall was on the great hall and Mhairi could not hear any conversation there as she left the solar with Genevieve. It was usually quiet in the morning, while the men went about their chores. The activity was in the kitchen before the midday meal.

She halted on the landing on the floor below, as if intending to go into the chamber she shared with Eglantine. "I thank you for your assistance this day," she said to the healer, who smiled.

"I suspect Talbot had the greater challenge in the falconry. The birds were agitated indeed." The older woman touched Mhairi's arm. "She is fine."

Mhairi nodded agreement and waited on the

landing until the healer was out of sight. She counted to a hundred to give Genevieve time to cross the hall, then descended with care.

The hall was empty, just as she had anticipated. She crossed it quickly and silently, ducking into the bailey. She clung to the shadows as she made her way to the stables, ensuring that no one saw her enter.

Quentin would be given a pallet over the stables. It was where all male guests who were not noble were invited to sleep. The smith was at his forge, his boy fetching water for him, and a palfrey in need of a shoe tethered beside him. Two men gossiped beside the smith, watching his work. The ostler was walking a destrier in the bailey, checking its gait, and Mhairi recognized the warhorse that had been limping of late.

She saw two boys carrying buckets of steaming water from the kitchens to the far end of the stables and guessed where she would find Quentin. The Hawk's hospitality always included a hot bath for those who had journeyed far.

Mhairi looked left and right, ensuring that she was not observed, and silently crept closer.

CHAPTER TWO

he Hawk's hospitality was as generous as ever. There was ale and bread, both most welcome after Quentin's hungry days of travel. He was assigned a pallet in the stables and offered a bath, two welcome luxuries he had not experienced in a while. He recognized many in the service of the Hawk, men who had once answered to him as Captain of the Guard, but he avoided them on purpose. They were trained to be observant and the most likely to notice that his injuries were less than he implied.

He sighed with relief when he entered the bathing chamber at the very end of the stables. There was straw underfoot and bales of hay stacked in one corner. The shadows were deep despite the hour and the scent of horses was strong. A large tub filled with hot water was in the middle of what had once been two stalls. A boy emptied a bucket of water into the tub, then bobbed his head at Quentin before seizing his two empty buckets and retreating. There was a piece of rough soap and a thick cloth and Quentin eyed both with gratitude.

He shut the wooden portal with some effort, for it clearly had not been closed in a while, then secured it. He reached to unfasten his cloak, and that was when he knew he was not alone.

He could hear someone breathing.

The hair prickled on the back of his neck, awareness sending a welcome surge through him. He was immediately as alert as a hound on a scent.

There was only one place to hide and that was behind the bales of hay. Quentin continued to fuss with his robe, as if he had trouble unfastening it, and hobbled closer to that corner. He heard a slight movement, then deliberately turned his back on that corner. He pretended to be absorbed in the matter of his clasp and muttered beneath his breath in apparent frustration.

The other person moved, taking a stealthy step closer.

Someone he had trained. The pause between steps was long, just as he instructed, and their timing was irregular.

Surely it could not be *her*. His heart rose to his throat.

The person stepped closer, the faintest rustle of straw revealing a step, then abruptly reached for him.

Quentin felt the movement of air because he was waiting for it.

And he moved faster. He spun and snatched, locking his damaged hand around the throat of his assailant and backing that person into the wall. Mhairi stared back at him as he held her there, her gaze unflinching, fairly daring him to squeeze the life out of her.

Mhairi.

"Not so feeble as that," she whispered, and her eyes began to twinkle.

Quentin stepped back and turned away from her, trying to hide his pleasure. He forced himself to hobble, disgusted that he had revealed himself to her—and pleased at the same time that she had not been deceived after all. "It was luck," he said grimly.

"It was skill," she replied with the confidence he recalled. "You taught me the difference. You knew not only that I was here, but guessed my height and position. You made one strike and caught me by the throat, immobilizing me immediately." He stole a glance at her and she smiled at him. "I am glad indeed that you no longer possess a knife."

"You should not be here," he said, fighting his mixed feelings. How could he be both disgruntled and delighted?

"Neither should you," she said, stepping away from the wall and folding her arms across her chest. "I did not know he had sworn to have you killed if you returned."

"I suspect neither of us wanted you to know."

"But you risked that fate to keep a promise to me?"

"What if he killed me?" Quentin flung out a hand. "I will be a beggar until the end of my days, reliant upon the charity of others. My life is worthless now."

"You do not believe that," Mhairi said with curious conviction. She watched him closely. "You were filled with anger when you arrived, but it changes to despair."

"What would you know of it?"

"I know more than you think."

He pivoted to challenge her. "Then why do you think I came to Inverfyre?"

She bit her lip, considering him. "I would like to think that you came to see me again. I have thought of you every night and day since your departure and had hoped you might send word that you were well."

There was no accusation in her tone and no shyness in confessing her hopes. She was as honest as he recalled and Quentin found himself enchanted all over again.

How he wished he could be the man she desired.

"I wanted to return in triumph," he confessed, without having had any intention of doing so. "I wanted to offer you more than a knife that I could have given you seven years ago." Quentin sighed, then gestured impatiently at the bath. "The water cools and someone will hear us. You should leave."

Mhairi shook her head. "Not until you tell me

why you saved my mother."

"Why not? I have no argument with the lady."

"But you have one with my father, and anyone of sense in Inverfyre knows that the surest way to deal him a blow would be to hurt my mother. If she had died this day, it would have taken all the merit from his life."

"You assume much in thinking I wish him ill."

She took a step away from the wall, coming closer, and Quentin's mouth went dry at the recollection of her soft skin beneath his hand just moments before. "You were angry," she reminded him with conviction. "You came to Inverfyre, driven by that anger. I can only reason that you came to avenge yourself upon my father for what you have endured. If he had not expelled you from Inverfyre, you would not have been robbed and injured."

"Maimed," he corrected.

Mhairi's lashes swept down, hiding her thoughts, and he knew he had never seen a sight more alluring. "As you say," she murmured and he wondered how much of the truth she had guessed. "And so you might blame him for your fate."

He caught his breath but did not reply. She had always been too astute. "I say again, you assume much..."

"A warrior's code can be a harsh one. An eye for an eye. A death for a death." Her gaze swept over him and he was surprised to find no pity in her steady gaze. "But I had a good teacher once who

31

taught me that a man's true merit is never changed, regardless of what he has endured."

"Your teacher was a fool!" Quentin spat, knowing full well that she referred to him.

Mhairi shook her head. "He said the instinct is true and that when a warrior follows his intuitive reaction, his true nature is revealed. You saved my mother from injury, apparently without thinking that you might take the arrow instead. It was a selfless choice, one characteristic of the warrior I knew, and one that tells me you do not truly wish to injure my father."

Quentin was shaken by her perceptiveness. "Or it was a ruse to gain access to the keep," he muttered.

Mhairi smiled, unconvinced. "I think then that there would have been a moment's hesitation, based upon my teacher's instruction." When Quentin did not reply—for he agreed with her—she came to his side and placed her hand upon his arm. He felt her touch to his very toes, even through his cloak, and closed his eyes lest she discern his thoughts. "My teacher was a man of honor, a man who found opportunity in challenge, a man whose word could be relied upon."

Her conviction of his character was humbling, particularly as Quentin no longer believed that to be his measure. "The teacher you knew might as well be dead," he said, his words unexpectedly husky.

"Nay," she said, reaching to frame his face in her hands. "He is wounded. He feels he has been betrayed. It would only be reasonable to be angry. But the truth that he has forgotten is that he is loved, not for his hands and not for his eyes, but for the valor of his heart." She smiled a little. "He forgot that his gesture would reveal his nature."

And before Quentin could argue with her, she reached up and touched her lips to his.

It was a kiss that undid him completely. It was a kiss he had intended to steal but which was offered freely; a kiss that shattered the last of his bitterness and dispelled it; a kiss that kindled that valor he had nigh forgotten he possessed.

For with her kiss, Mhairi not only reminded Quentin of the man he used to be, but awakened within him the desire to be that man once more.

❧

Quentin fairly flung her out of the chamber when he suddenly ended their kiss, and Mhairi was too overwhelmed by his touch to argue with him. She had sensed the fury within him at the gates, but recognized that his attitude had already changed. She had little time to measure his mood before the door was closed against her, but could not dismiss her sense that his anger had changed its focus.

She paused outside the chamber, leaning back against the wall to catch her breath, and listened to him splash in the water. She would have given much to see him nude, and not just to satisfy her curiosity about the extent of his injuries.

The very force and speed with which Quentin

had evicted her revealed that he was not as feeble as he would have all believe.

She smiled, gladdened by that, then sobered at a thought. She had never asked him how he had anticipated the MacLarens' assault. How much did he know of their plans? She recalled his suggestion that his choice might have been a ruse and chilled. Surely he was not allied with the MacLarens?

Surely he was not a spy for them within Inverfyre's walls?

Surely the Quentin she knew could never be so traitorous?

But there was his anger...

Mhairi glanced over her shoulder to the chamber, wanting to know the truth. She tried the door quietly but it was bolted from the other side.

"I will only be a moment longer," Quentin growled, clearly thinking another wished to bathe.

She put her lips to the crack in the wood. "Take your leisure," she whispered. "I will see you at the board this night."

The sound of water stilled as if she had shocked him, but Mhairi spied a stable hand approaching. She retreated into the shadows and took the long way around the bailey, pausing in the armory for a moment, then talking to the cook. She walked the battlements and found Nigel there, surveying the forests, and behaved as if she had just come from their mother's side.

All the while, her thoughts were churning. Would she have another chance to speak to

Quentin?

Would she have another kiss?

Even as she tasted him upon her lips, Mhairi knew she wanted more, far more, than one more kiss.

If Quentin had felt at odds before, Mhairi's kiss only made the matter worse. Or was it her confidence in him that shook him so?

What was his path, if not to avenge himself upon the Hawk?

How could he show himself as the man Mhairi believed him to be?

Certainly not by avenging himself upon her father.

What if he could prove his merit? Might the Hawk welcome his service again? His injuries were less than he let them believe, but his hand was still marred. Hope lit in Quentin's heart, a sense that had become unfamiliar to him, but was welcome all the same.

He stared at the ceiling from his pallet as he considered what little he had overheard in the forest the night before. The MacLarens had meant to assault Lady Aileen this day. They said it would be a sign to their man within the walls of Inverfyre. Quentin wished he had heard more.

Who was the traitor in the Hawk's court?

Could he reveal the spy and win the laird's favor?

Quentin fell asleep on the straw pallet after his bath with his thoughts spinning. He was lulled by the sound of the horses below and the familiar rhythm of Inverfyre, the recollection dawning within him of how much he had loved this place. He slept more deeply than he might have expected, but then, it was the first time Quentin had felt safe in seven years.

Aye, Inverfyre was the place he had long felt to be home.

After Mhairi's kiss, though, he felt that he owed the Hawk thanks for letting him know it at all, never mind for allowing him to return, even if only for one night.

Perhaps his anger had served its purpose in driving him back to the place he had long considered to be home.

Perhaps his return meant his heart could be healed.

❧

Quentin awakened to find the sky darkening and the new ostler calling to him from below. "Hoy, there! Do you mean to share the evening meal?"

Quentin thanked the man and donned his boots, then walked to the hall behind the others. He deliberately made slow progress and expected he would find only a place at the back of the hall. It would be a good place to observe the others and seek changes in them, changes that might reveal their alliances.

The Hawk met him at the door to the hall, though. If his manner was cool, Quentin could not blame him and he admired the older man's grace.

"My guest," the Hawk said. "Come to the high table, Quentin, that I might properly thank you for your action this day."

"It is not necessary," Quentin objected, seeing that three of the Hawk's children and his wife were already seated at the high table.

"It *is* necessary," the Hawk insisted, then dropped his voice. His gaze was steely. "All must see that my debts are paid."

Of course. This was the ethical man he recalled and whom he had been proud to serve.

Quentin nodded and continued to the high table in the Hawk's company, well aware that every gaze in the hall followed his progress. He heard the whispers and ignored them. It was only right that some doubted his objectives, even if the Hawk hid his own doubts.

Quentin sought the changes. The Hawk and Aileen's two younger sons must have finally been sent away to train for their spurs. Quentin calculated as he walked. Gawain must be nigh grown to manhood by now, and Avery not far behind him. He had begun their training and wondered if they thought of him at all.

Nigel, the Hawk's eldest son and heir, was a fine young knight, dark of hair and blue of eye. Quentin's reckoning made him twenty-two summers of age and he saw how the son favored the father in appearance. Was his nature similar, too? Quentin did not know Nigel well, for the boy had been training for his spurs when Quentin had arrived at Inverfyre and had only returned home for occasional visits. Where had the boy trained? Quentin could not recall the name of the holding. His patron had been a cousin on his mother's side in England.

Evangeline, the Hawk's second child, had blossomed into the raven-haired beauty all had anticipated she would become. She undoubtedly would be some man's prized bride, though she was the kind of woman whose company left Quentin tongue-tied. He supposed her marriage had been arranged, and realized with some discomfiture that Mhairi's might be as well.

He had no right to have any hopes, but realized that he did.

The Hawk matched his pace to Quentin's slower one, but did not otherwise aid him. In a way, Quentin was grateful for that. In another, it foiled his attempt to appear to be a cripple. He stumbled on purpose, but the Hawk merely steadied his elbow with a touch, then let him continue alone.

"I have a favor to ask of you," the Hawk said in an undertone.

"Indeed?"

"I would hear what you know of the MacLaren clan and how you anticipated them this day."

Quentin had anticipated the question and nodded agreement. "The better to rout them," he said.

The Hawk met his gaze steadily. "There will be no second instance of this day's events."

"I recall that you do not suffer an error twice."

Their gazes met and held. "Indeed," the Hawk said tightly. "I will speak to you after the meal, when there are fewer listening ears."

"Of course." Quentin deliberately did not call the Hawk his lord, and knew the omission was noted.

"I hope you enjoy the fare." The Hawk indicated an empty place at the end of the high table before taking his own seat.

Quentin's spot was at the opposite end from Mhairi. She was watching him and he held her gaze for a potent moment as he recalled that unexpected kiss. Even the memory sent heat flooding through him, but he dropped his gaze that no others might see. He bowed to her father and took his place beside Evangeline, who spared him a glance filled with pity.

Ahearn O'Donnell, a comrade of the Hawk's, arrived in that moment and took the seat on Quentin's other side. Quentin noted that Ahearn's handshake was as resolute as before and it appeared the man had lost none of his easy charm.

Reinhard took the place at the far end of the table, beside Mhairi, pausing to spare a glance of open suspicion at Quentin. The Hawk was seated in the middle, his wife on his left and his heir on his right. Squires stood behind every second person, prepared to serve. The linen on the board was simple but finely wrought. The torches burned bright and the fire was lit on the hearth. Dogs slept in the rushes at the back of the hall, and those men invited to dine in the lord's hall chatted easily to each other. There was trust, and honor, and security in this hall.

God's wounds, but he had loved this place and the people within it. Quentin surveyed the hall and thought time might have stood still.

Save for his injuries.

Save for the silver at Ahearn's temples, the lines on Reinhard's face, and the winter on the Hawk's brow. He was not the sole one who had changed in seven years, but he was the one who had let his experiences betray his nature.

Mhairi's kiss reminded him that he owed better than that to all he knew.

Regardless of what his own future might be.

In that moment, Quentin decided that he would leave a legacy of merit, despite his injuries. He knew then that he would do whatever was necessary to aid the Hawk in ridding his forests of the MacLarens. They were the vermin who threatened this haven.

They were more deserving recipients of his fury.

The Hawk raised his cup and saluted the gathering. The company raised their cups in turn and drank to their laird's good health. The Hawk smiled, then beckoned to the cook and the first dish was carried from the kitchens to be served. Chatter erupted throughout the hall as the smell of the food filled the air.

"I suppose we have all changed in your absence," Ahearn said as a fine rabbit stew was ladled on to the trencher they would share. It was like the man to put another at ease and Quentin nodded.

"I was thinking Inverfyre was much the same," he admitted.

"Truly?" Ahearn grinned. "Though I become a greybeard, and the children have grown so tall?"

"The Hawk's children? Or have your own?"

"They have all grown like weeds in the sun." Ahearn granted Quentin a quick look. "And you? Do you miss it?"

There was no harm in admitting the truth. "Who would not miss a holding so justly governed and prosperous?" Quentin asked. "Inverfyre was the finest place I ever served." He glanced around. "It is good to find it so much the same."

Ahearn nodded. "And what will you do now?"

"I am uncertain," Quentin said, for it was true. He did not know if his aid would be welcome as yet. Reinhard's expression indicated otherwise and he had the thought that the Hawk had been strategic in more than the seating.

Reinhard evidently was the skeptical one, while Ahearn the apparent friend. No doubt between the two men, the Hawk hoped to discern the truth of Quentin's intentions in returning to Inverfyre.

The stew was beguiling, so rich and thick with meat, so savory that Quentin nigh wept with the pleasure of eating it. He had survived upon stale bread and foraged berries for too long. "I dared not think beyond arriving here," he confessed to Ahearn.

"And keeping your pledge to Mhairi," Ahearn said. "That was a fine impulse, to be sure." He inhaled the scent of the egg dish offered to them, his appreciation clear.

"And where are the others so loyal to the Hawk?" Quentin asked. "Is Fernando no longer in your ranks?"

Ahearn granted him an assessing glance. "Of course."

"Yet he is not at the board."

"Someone must watch the gates," Ahearn said with care. "Someone trusted by the Hawk." He raised his brows. "If naught else, you owe the MacLaren clan your thanks this day."

"How so?"

"Their attack and your intervention have together ensured that you are guest instead of villain returned. How did you know their intent?"

Quentin heard the implication in the other man's tone, as if he might have convinced the MacLaren clan to attack on this very morning for his own purposes. Perhaps Ahearn shared Reinhard's doubts.

"I may not be considered the villain returned, though it is clear my motives are yet suspect," he noted.

Ahearn shook a finger at him, pretending to tease but Quentin saw that he made no jest. "It was you who taught me to distrust coincidence."

"And there is only my word that it was not," Quentin acknowledged. "That doubt is fair." He became aware that Evangeline was listening avidly to their conversation. "What little I know will be confided at the Hawk's invitation alone."

Ahearn nodded approval of that. "Well, I must ensure that you know all the doings of this place!" he said heartily. "You will want to know who has had children and who has left this world. Let me fatigue you with all the tidings of the village."

Quentin nodded agreement, well aware that the other man had turned the discussion to matters other than the defense of Inverfyre.

He was not trusted, though he was within the hall.

Evangeline sighed and rolled her eyes. "I would prefer to hear all of the world beyond Inverfyre's borders."

"I have little good to tell of it," Quentin said, but she still looked discontent.

"At least Gawain and Avery were allowed to go to Ravensmuir," she said. "I scarce leave the walls of Inverfyre!"

"Because you do not care to hunt, my lady," Ahearn reminded her gently.

She rolled her eyes. "It matters little now. No one will hunt until Papa decides the forest is safe."

It was true enough.

Ahearn leaned close. "Reinhard there has another young babe," he said with a smile. "And a surprise she was to both himself and Margery."

Reinhard and Margery had four sons, who had been born in rapid succession after their nuptials. Even when Quentin had left, the youngest had been ten summers of age. "So long after their boys? That would be a surprise."

Ahearn chuckled. "I told him that I thought he should know by this point what causes his wife's belly to round." Quentin smiled, for Ahearn had always been quick to tease his fellows. "And she is a pretty lass. You will see how her father dotes upon her."

As Ahearn satisfied Quentin's curiosity, Evangeline sighed and turned to her mother for conversation.

Mhairi, Quentin noticed, was yet watching him. She was not for him. He could not be for her. But fool that he was, her attention warmed his heart.

He did not doubt that the Hawk had noted her interest as well.

❧

The seating arrangement at the high table was not a coincidence.

Mhairi knew her father well enough to understand that Quentin had been placed as far away from her as possible, in order to ensure that she had no chance to talk to him.

44

Usually, Ahearn or Fernando sat between her and Reinhard, because her father kept all the unwed men in the keep away from Evangeline. That he had changed his scheme told her that her father had discerned her affection for Quentin.

And deliberately thwarted it.

Annoyance rose hot within her, followed quickly by rebellion. She must find a way to speak to Quentin again, even if her father meant to keep them apart.

"You were always one to hope for the impossible," Nigel said under his breath and she knew her reaction showed.

"There is nothing wrong with having aspirations," Mhairi replied. She and her oldest brother seldom agreed, so it did not surprise her to be chastised by him.

"But you are the daughter of Inverfyre," Nigel continued quietly. "You have a responsibility to wed well. Surely you understand that your marriage should bring a benefit to the holding?" He spared a glance at Quentin, his meaning so clear that Mhairi bristled.

"Just because a man has been injured does not make him worthless."

Nigel raised his brows and said nothing.

"Your fate does not have to be mine," Mhairi argued. "I am third. You and Evangeline can manage the strategic alliances and I will wed for love."

Nigel laughed outright. "No one of sense weds

for love, Mhairi! I thought you more clever than that!"

"Our parents love each other."

"Yet their match began with an abduction. Love came later, as is right and good."

"And if it had not?"

"They would still be wedded, and undoubtedly, still be happy together. It is Inverfyre that is of greatest import and they have built a strong legacy together. They would both have satisfaction in that achievement, even if they were not smitten with each other."

Mhairi wished she could remain silent but she could not. Nigel was simply too convinced of his own perspective. "I would argue that Papa recognized his true love on sight, and that was why he stole Maman."

Nigel chuckled. "Not just love but love at a glimpse? Who knew such fanciful notions filled your thoughts? I would never have thought it of you."

"It is not whimsy!"

"So, you yearn for Quentin because you imagine your affection for him is destined to be?" Nigel shook his head, not waiting for her reply. "Believe what you must, sister mine." He slanted a teasing glance her way. "I supposed I should be reassured that you possess *some* feminine whimsy. Otherwise it might seem I had another brother."

"There are days when I wish you did," Mhairi said under her breath.

"Why?"

"Because you can do as you wish."

Nigel laughed again. "Where do you think I learned this notion of responsibility? What I wish is for Inverfyre to prosper, which means that my desires must be for the good of the holding, not fleeting urges. I learned young that my own desires were nothing if they did not ally with the needs of Inverfyre." Nigel urged a choice piece of venison toward her. "Be glad that you were not born first, Mhairi. And savor the meat, for there may be less of it in the near future."

Mhairi saw then how much her brother resembled their father, for his expression was uncommonly stern and his words revealed that he, too, had concluded that no one would ride to hunt soon.

"I would hunt."

"You know it will not be permitted."

"Then what is to be done?"

Nigel gave her a steady look. "I have no doubt the threat will be removed, and then you can ride to hunt again."

Nigel and their father would see the MacLarens routed, it was clear. "Perhaps Quentin will provide tidings of aid in that. Perhaps you will then see his merit."

"Perhaps the challenge will be to judge his trustworthiness," Nigel said beneath his breath then gestured for Mhairi to leave the matter be. A squire approached with another platter, one that smelled of apples, and she bit her tongue with frustration.

She would defend Quentin, even if she was the sole one to do as much.

Could she help with Inverfyre's retaliation against the MacLarens?

Her father would protest against it, but perhaps Quentin would argue her merit. He had always believed in her skills. Her heart glowed in recollection of his praise earlier this day and she flushed a little in memory of that kiss. She resisted the urge to finger the hilt of the knife he had given to her. She watched him covertly, noting that although his body had been damaged, his nature was as constant as ever.

He spoke little.

He listened intently.

He glanced frequently over the hall, and she did not doubt that he could give an inventory of who was present and who had spoken to whom.

He kept his own counsel and she suspected it was as good as ever.

When he smiled at a comment Ahearn made, she caught a glimpse of his former self. Her heart clenched tightly at the damage he had endured.

Then he looked down the table, his gaze colliding suddenly with her own. He must have discerned something in her expression, for he scowled, shook his head minutely and turned back to Ahearn.

Mhairi felt as if she had been chided.

But she would not allow him to dismiss her as

readily as that.

CHAPTER THREE

fter the meal, the Hawk beckoned to Quentin, no doubt so they would speak in more private quarters. Already the knights and men-at-arms in the Hawk's service turned to their games of chance, while those from the village who had come to the hall for the meal rose to return home. Quentin felt Ahearn's presence behind him and noted that he had been positioned between the two men, where he could be more readily observed.

The sign of distrust was not unexpected, but it hampered any notion he had to be of aid to the Hawk and Inverfyre. He could tell them any detail and might not be believed. Who was the MacLaren spy within the walls? Would the Hawk even believe there was one?

He recalled his own lessons about using

opposition instead of battling against it, and considered other possibilities. If he fed the doubts of the Hawk's trusted advisors and was cast out of Inverfyre, he could perhaps pretend to ally himself with the MacLarens and spy upon their plans. He might then be in the best position to foil them.

Still, Quentin would prefer to confide in the Hawk, to be trusted and remain within the walls to battle for justice.

The Hawk looked back and Quentin saw both Nigel and Reinhard rise to their feet. Mhairi looked as if she were itching to do the same, but Quentin averted his gaze from hers again and saw Lady Aileen speak to her daughter. Mhairi remained at the board, displeasure in her expression. Evangeline conferred with her maid about some frippery or other while Lady Aileen smiled upon those remaining in the hall. Her eyes were bright and he knew she would not miss any detail.

'Twas a fine thing that the Hawk's wife watched his back and Quentin had always admired their marriage. There had been a time when he had aspired to claiming a wife of similar valor and sense, though he knew the chance of his wedding now was so low as to be non-existent. He had no means of seeing a family fed, to be sure.

The men entered the small room where the Hawk kept his accounts, the castellan, Henry, securing the door behind them—and doubtless standing guard.

There was only a single lantern burning on the

table in the middle of the chamber, placed there by Henry in anticipation of their arrival. The Hawk sat in his great chair and Nigel leaned against the opposite wall, his arms folded across his chest. His eyes were narrowed and he was watchful. Quentin liked that the boy was observant and slow to reveal his thoughts. He would make a good laird, like his father.

Reinhard crouched, as was his way, head bowed as he listened. He seldom missed a detail, which Quentin admired, too. Ahearn braced his hands upon his hips and stood beside Quentin, his position feeding Quentin's notion that he was being guarded.

Indeed, he could fairly taste the distrust of the Hawk's men. It surrounded Quentin like wood smoke—pervasive and impossible to ignore. They would not be readily convinced of his innocence.

Still, he would try before he changed plans.

The Hawk himself was as inscrutable as ever, but Reinhard wore his suspicion boldly for all to see. He refused to even shake Quentin's hand. "You knew of their scheme," he said by way of greeting. "Did you foil it or were you part of it?"

How like Reinhard to slice directly to the meat of the matter. "I overheard them, three nights ago," Quentin said. He meant to stand, but at the Hawk's gesture, he sat on a bench, his hands braced on his cane.

Let them think him more feeble than he was.

"Three nights?" Reinhard said. "And yet you

brought no warning! What if you had not aided the lady in time!"

The Hawk raised a hand for silence. "Save your questions until Quentin has shared his tale." He nodded at Quentin. "Tell us first what happened to you."

"I was robbed in Spain and fool enough to fight the thieves. They ensured I could not pursue them, and perhaps intended that I would not be able to identify them." He touched his eye patch.

"You had a destrier from Ravensmuir, but you arrived here on foot," Ahearn noted.

"I believe it was Tyr that first attracted their avarice," Quentin admitted, his heart heavy. He would never come to terms with that loss and regularly worried that the stallion had been injured or abandoned. His throat was tight when he spoke. "They surrounded me and cut his flank, not deeply but enough to spook him. When he threw me, they seized him and his trap, plus my armor, my boots and my coin. They left me to die, with only my chemise." He forced a wry smile. "Perhaps it was not clean enough to tempt them."

"But you did *not* die," Reinhard noted, clearly doubting the tale. "Perhaps this is a ruse, and your belongings are at a tavern in Glasgow or Carlisle. Perhaps you came to Inverfyre for vengeance!"

Quentin met Reinhard's gaze and refused to let his anger show. "A monk found me and showed me compassion, taking me to a hospital and paying for my care. I made the pilgrimage to Compostela in the company of Brother Guillaume and his fellows."

"And then you came here," Nigel said, his words quiet.

"To keep my promise to your sister, aye."

Reinhard arched a brow, inviting the details.

"Before I left, I vowed to bring her a knife with a blade of Toledo steel. She is a valiant warrior in her own right, and I knew she would treasure a weapon of merit. That promise was the sole deed unfinished in my life, so I returned to keep my vow."

Reinhard snorted at that. "And your timing was so perfect that you heard the scheme of the MacLarens just before it was launched. I say you lie."

Ahearn cleared his throat. "He did ask about the warriors missing from the hall at the evening meal."

"The better to assess Inverfyre's strength?" Nigel asked, his gaze was considering. He did not seem to expect an answer, so Quentin did not give him one.

The tension was thick in the chamber.

"What of the blade you gave to Mhairi?" Ahearn asked. "I thought I recognized it as the one you had before."

"If you were robbed as you say, why would they leave you with such a fine blade?" Reinhard asked. "It would fetch a good price anywhere."

"I fell upon it when attacked, hiding it from my assailants." Quentin shrugged. "Perhaps it, too, had sufficient need of a polish that they underestimated its worth. I chose to believe that it had been left with me and that I had survived so that I might keep my promise to Mhairi. This was Brother Guillaume's assessment of God's will."

Again there was a heavy silence and the air seemed thick with unspoken accusations.

"Tell us what you learned of the MacLarens," the Hawk invited after several moments.

"I slept in the forest, every night of my journey north," Quentin said. "If I wrap myself in my cloak and find a hollow, I am nigh invisible in the darkness. At least now, I escape the attention of bandits and thieves. Three nights past, when I approached Inverfyre, I heard the whispers."

"From which direction did you approach?" Reinhard asked without looking up.

"The southwest. I took the road from Glasgow, then crossed the Rannoch Moor."

"A hard journey," Reinhard noted, granting Quentin a piercing glance. "You could have taken the road from the east and had an easier walk."

Quentin's gaze did not waver. "I have learned to avoid the busier thoroughfares. There are those who believe invalids make easy prey."

"Two and a half days' walk would put you well beyond Inverfyre's boundaries," Reinhard noted. "So far that it seems unlikely you would find any MacLarens conspiring there. Even at your current pace, you must make at least ten miles a day."

"That is true enough," Quentin acknowledged. "I was close to Inverfyre's gates three days ago. It

55

was falling dark. I planned to sleep, then approach the keep in the morning."

"You would sleep in the forest instead of in the hall?" Reinhard demanded.

"I would be rested to better argue my case," Quentin said and felt their suspicion redouble. "I was uncertain of my reception."

"Fair enough," Ahearn murmured.

"Where did you sleep?" Reinhard asked.

"South of the line of silver trees. I headed into the forest and found a hollow that was dry."

The Hawk's gaze brightened but then he dropped his gaze, hiding his interest. Did he know the spot?

"And did you sleep well?"

"I might have, but I heard whispers. They were three. I could not see them, but heard their voices. I dared not move to a better vantage point lest I be revealed."

"You would not have seen daylight then, were they MacLarens," Reinhard muttered.

Quentin nodded. "They spoke of Caillen's legacy, and that Christmas would be celebrated with him being made Laird of Inverfyre."

"Caillen MacLaren?" the Hawk asked, looking at Ahearn. Quentin understood that that man had the best understanding of the Hawk's opponents.

"Oldest son of Hamish, who is himself the first cousin of Dubhglas. Hamish has raised his sons with a harsh hand and a lust for vengeance. They are cruel, impulsive and unafraid to shed blood."

"All because I killed Dubhglas," the Hawk murmured. "Yet I have never regretted the deed." He drummed his fingers. "And so the battle for Inverfyre is renewed."

"They said they would slaughter the witch of Inverfyre first," Quentin said. "I was not certain who they meant, not until their assault."

Unease slid around the chamber and the Hawk frowned. "Aileen is no witch," he said, but he spoke without his usual conviction.

"Yet, evidently she is believed to be one by the MacLarens," Quentin said. "They referred to an ally within the walls who would admit them in the night, so they could claim Inverfyre from within."

"Who?"

"They did not say."

"When?" Reinhard demanded.

Quentin shrugged. "They did not say."

The Captain of the Guard's lips tightened in dissatisfaction and his suspicion visibly grew. "You simply tell us only part of the truth, in order to bait a trap," he said. "You would feed suspicion between us to divert it from yourself. We know each other here! You are the stranger." The Hawk again waved for silence. Reinhard paced the width of the chamber and back, fairly growling with annoyance.

"If they have an ally, who might it be?" Nigel asked calmly. "Are there any men at Inverfyre we do not trust fully? Are there any new arrivals within the walls?"

Reinhard shook his head, resolute. "There is

only one newly arrived," he growled.

Quentin was aware that they all avoided his gaze. They would never trust him. His choice was made.

"And now your promise is kept," Reinhard said crisply. "How soon will you depart?"

Quentin recognized his moment. "I had hoped to stay," he declared, his tone challenging. "I had hoped to find service here again."

"In your maimed state?" Reinhard demanded. "What could you do, Quentin? You are no longer an able warrior, and this tale of yours invites doubt, if not more. I will have no man in service at Inverfyre who I cannot rely upon completely, not when the MacLarens muster outside our very gates!"

"And you do not trust me so?" Quentin asked, his tone provocative. He rose to his feet, leaning more heavily upon his cane than was necessary.

"Why should I?" Reinhard asked. "You openly defied the Hawk and were cast out for your audacity. Now you return, bitter, marred and clearly still smitten with the daughter of the house who was too far above you when you were able. Why did you return? It cannot be out of goodwill." He jabbed a finger through the air at Quentin. "You came for vengeance! You came to steal Mhairi away! And I doubt you would shirk from betraying the Hawk, given what you have endured!"

Quentin took a step forward. "Then why would I have intervened for Lady Aileen this day?"

"To pursue your suit!" Reinhard roared, stepped forward so they were toe to toe. "To try to prove your merit. But I know your merit, Quentin, and I knew it seven years ago." He poked Quentin in the shoulder, hard. Quentin stumbled backward though he could have held his ground. "No warrior of merit defies his lord's command."

"Not even to train a warrior of promise? One who begs for instruction? One with a natural gift that cannot be denied?"

"It was not your choice!" Reinhard roared. "Your role was to *obey*!" He gave Quentin a push and Quentin lost his balance on purpose, stumbling into the bench and upsetting it.

"I regret nothing," he said with heat. "I made a promise. I returned to keep it." He turned to the Hawk, who was watching with interest. "If you do not trust me, cast me from your gates, along with all the other refuse within your walls."

The Hawk held Quentin's gaze for a long moment, as if he did not share Reinhard's view of Quentin's nature. He nodded once before abruptly rising to his feet, his decision made. "I would ask you to depart in the morning, at first light." He offered his hand. "You have my best wishes for your future."

And so the Hawk would show him mercy again. Quentin refused to be vexed by the courtesy he did not desire.

Nay, he knew how best to provoke the Laird of Inverfyre, for he had done as much before.

Mhairi's curiosity burned with the need to be satisfied. What did Quentin know? Did her father believe him? What would be his fate?

She waited until Evangeline finally dozed off, even letting her sister claim more of the pelts in their chamber than usual. When Evangeline was cold, she did not sleep and Mhairi wanted her sister to sleep as soon as possible. It was irksome indeed that on this night of nights, Evangeline was talkative. She speculated on Quentin's intentions and insisted on seeing the knife he had given to Mhairi. She wondered aloud about her own marital prospects, and shared her concerns about their mother. She asked Mhairi how she thought their father would retrieve the *Titulus Croce* from the priory in time for the Mass on Sunday, and Mhairi did not reply. It was only when she pretended to sleep and was utterly silent that her sister's chatter finally faded.

As soon as Evangeline was breathing deeply, Mhairi slipped from her own pallet and moved silently to the door. She went down the stairs as quietly as a shadow, and noted the silence of the hall. If all had retired, she would have to go to the stables to talk to Quentin. Could she manage to do as much unobserved twice in one day?

She drew the knife that Quentin had given her, liking the weight of it in her hand.

She paused at the foot of the stairs at the rumble of men's voices and peeked into the quiet hall. The torches were being extinguished and the food had been cleared. The trestle tables were folded against the walls and the older maid from the kitchens was sweeping the rushes away. A pair of hunting dogs chewed bones by the fire, which had burned down to embers, and Mhairi knew they were only there because her mother was not present to shoo them out to the stables. Ahearn's sons were still in one corner, playing dice, but the other men had left the hall.

The voices she heard came from the men emerging from her father's chamber. Henry was first, carrying a lantern for her father and brother. With a word, they departed for her father's final inspection of the ramparts, Reinhard fast behind them. They did not even glance back at the rest of the party.

Her heart leaped when Quentin hobbled into view. Ahearn strode past him without a word, beckoning to his sons. The boys roused themselves and hastened after their father, whose home was in the village.

Quentin was alone. He surveyed the hall, as if to memorize it, then considered the path that Reinhard had taken with the Hawk and Nigel. When he took a step toward the stairs, Mhairi knew his intent.

She swallowed and stepped out of the shadows, revealing her presence to him. His expression lit and she was thrilled that he strode directly toward her. It seemed to her that he stood straighter and walked with greater purpose.

What had her father said to him?

What had he asked of her father?

Quentin paused before her, scarcely leaning on his cane at all, reinforcing her suspicion that his injuries were less than he let others believe. He glanced down at the knife in her hand and nodded. "So, you like it."

"I always liked it." She swallowed. "I have fine memories of it, and of the man who wielded it. Are you certain you do not need it?"

Quentin gave her an intent look then lifted his damaged hand. "My days of warfare are over."

"Does it hurt?"

"No longer," he admitted and she liked that he was still honest with her. Quentin had never protected her from the truth, even when she might not like it. "I imagine sometimes that I can feel the finger yet, though it is long gone. It is curious." He nodded. "I miss the eye most, for its loss ensures my vulnerability on that side." His gaze slid to hers. "And I miss the sense of my own invincibility, though clearly, that was a lie."

"I wish you had not left Inverfyre."

"Because then I would not have been robbed?"

"And injured, and cheated."

"Aye, I thought as much when I was left to die." Quentin frowned and nodded. "But now, I am no longer sure one leads to the other. I might have been robbed right here, in the forests of Inverfyre, and wounded even more grievously. I was a fighting man and a warrior, Mhairi. Dire injury is very oft a part of that trade."

She disliked that he spoke of his occupation as a matter of the past. "And now?"

"And now I have no good purpose."

"But still you have your skills. Still you could teach, or advise on matters of strategy."

"But I would have to be trusted for that, and I am not trusted at Inverfyre. If that will be my fate, it will not be achieved here."

"You are leaving."

"I am leaving. This time, I doubt that I will return."

"It is not fair!" Mhairi protested. "Papa should never have cast you out..."

Quentin shook his head. "He was in the right, Mhairi. Never forget that. I defied him. Twice." He smiled at her, his gaze alight. "Know that I would do it a third time, for you, but there is nothing to be gained from such a course."

"You could offer for me." Even as she said the words, she knew it was an impossible desire.

"Your father could not let any man in his service offer for his own daughter," Quentin chided quietly. "That was true seven years ago and is more true now. Think of the line that would form for Evangeline, then! And what of the life we might have led? A laird should be able to rely upon his daughter's husband, but to employ him? Nay, it would muddy matters overmuch, and there would inevitably be talk of favor shown where it was not deserved."

Mhairi could not help but be pleased that he did not dismiss her suggestion of marriage in its own right. "Then I was not alone in my regard?"

Quentin surveyed her. "Nay, Mhairi, you were but late to it, and young. I knew my place, and I knew the import of defying your father's command. Yet I cannot regret that I succumbed to your plea. I could have done nothing else when you entreated me to teach you more."

"Because I was a good student?"

"That, to be sure." His smile broadened. "But more importantly, because it was you." Their gazes clung for a potent moment and Mhairi could not draw a breath. Then Quentin averted his gaze and frowned. "And so it was that when the Hawk chastised me, I did not argue with his decision. In his place, I knew I would have done the same—or even been more harsh. I saw it as an opportunity and an invitation."

"What happened?"

"I rode south to earn the coin I would need to ask honestly for your hand."

"Truly?"

"Truly. I am the fifth son of a younger son and there are no crumbs from my father's table for me. He saw me trained by my uncle, and ensured that I was outfitted well, and your father granted me a magnificent destrier. I had more, far more, than many other in my place, and I was confident I could succeed."

She waited when he fell silent.

"The tragedy of it is that I did succeed," Quentin admitted quietly, then raised his gaze to hers. "I had the coin. I had earned sufficient, but I wanted just a measure more. My luck had been excellent, which should have warned me. Instead, it made me think I could not lose."

"Your coin was stolen," Mhairi said quietly.

"More than that. My coin, my horse, my armor and my sword, my dignity and my hope. I lost all that day on the road to Compostela, and was certain that death would be too good an end."

"But?" she prompted when he fell silent again.

"But a pilgrim found me, a monk, and took me to shelter and tended me. He bade me accompany him and his fellows to Compostela while I healed, and he reminded me that I had more than I realized. I was alive, and while injured, many of those wounds would heal. He taught me to find the merit even in my wretched state."

"We could still marry. We could flee together."

"Nay." He must have read her thoughts, for he raised a finger. "And not for a lack of desire on my part. I do not have the means, my lady, and I will never have them again. There was a moment, a short wondrous moment, in which it might have been possible, but that moment is gone and it is gone forever. I have nothing to offer you, and so I will ask only one thing of you. Know that I will not dishonor you."

She saw that he would not be swayed and his honor made her mourn what would never be theirs.

"My father..."

"Has done more than enough," Quentin said. "He has done far more than I would do in his place, to be sure." He leaned forward and covered his hand with hers for a thrilling moment. "He will wed you to a man of merit, a man who can care for you as you deserve, and he will ensure your future as I cannot."

"I would wed you."

"And you would regret it," Quentin whispered. "Let me remember you, looking at me as you do now, not with disdain or regret."

Mhairi's tears fell and she could not utter a word for her throat was tight. "What is this one gift you would have of me?" she whispered, for she would have given anything.

Quentin smiled slowly and she sensed that there was more to his request than he would confess to her in this moment. "Do you trust me?"

"Of course!"

"Then grant me one kiss, Mhairi, one kiss to heat my blood for all the rest of my days."

He wanted her to say farewell.

"One kiss," she whispered. "It is all I desire and yet so much less."

Quentin's gaze danced over her features with new intensity, then he dropped his walking stick and caught her face in his hands. His hands were warm, strong and gentle, his grip sure. He certainly did not waver on his feet. His gaze was steady, his scar not so fearsome as she might have thought, and the satisfaction in his smile made her heart thunder.

"Warrior maiden," he murmured. He gave her no opportunity to speak, but claimed her lips with his own. He slanted his mouth over hers and drew her close, deepening his kiss in a most satisfactory way.

Mhairi surrendered to his touch, reveling in this one moment. Quentin's touch felt strong and right, both possessive and gentle. She ran her hands over his shoulders, then slid her fingers into his hair, drawing him nearer, wanting more. She felt a molten heat inside herself and arched against him, wishing they might touch skin to skin. His tongue touched hers, sending fire through her, and she opened her mouth, inviting him to take all he desired of her.

She hoped Quentin's kiss would never end, but end it did and all too soon.

"Fiend!" her father cried, and Quentin released her abruptly. Mhairi glimpsed the satisfaction in his smile and the twinkle in his eye before he turned.

Had he anticipated this?

"Guards!" her father roared. "Cast this vermin from the gates with all haste!"

"Nay, Papa!" Mhairi cried, but Quentin moved away from her.

Nigel appeared from behind her father and grabbed her arm, holding her back when the mercenaries seized Quentin. They dragged him from the hall, having no care for his walking stick which was still at her feet. Quentin never glanced back, nor did he fight them. Mhairi bit back a cry.

"What will happen to him?" she whispered.

"Only what he deserves," her brother said. "You will remain here," he instructed, granting her a hard glare. Only when Mhairi nodded, knowing that resistance was futile, did he pick up the walking stick and march after the guards.

Or perhaps it was only because her father approached her. The Hawk came to stand beside Mhairi, his features as impassive as ever. "Your mother left you in the hall untended?" he asked.

"You know she did not," Mhairi said and spun to climb the stairs. "I wanted to see him again."

"And now you have," her father replied mildly.

Mhairi did not reply. She tasted Quentin's kiss again. There was nothing for it. She could not appreciate what she had and be content.

Why had he asked whether she trusted him?

Why had he been pleased to be interrupted?

Or had he been pleased to be thrown into the night? It made no sense, but Mhairi could not suppress the sense that Quentin had possessed a plan and she had aided him in its pursuit.

"And so you banished him, after all," Aileen said when the Hawk stepped into the solar. "Despite the fact that he saved my life this day."

There could be no question as to who she meant. The Hawk smiled a little, having expected no less of her than this challenge, and noted the answering flash in his wife's eyes. It was a blessing beyond compare that this woman was his partner and his love, and that the passion between them had only grown since they first had met. Her presence in his hall, her good sense in consultation, and the pleasure they found abed made the Hawk feel that he could conquer any challenge so long as his lady wife was by his side.

It shook him that he had nearly lost her this day, but he strove to hide his fear from her.

"I gave him what he desired of me, no more and no less," he said mildly.

"I do not understand."

"He sought an opportunity to prove himself, especially once it was clear that Reinhard doubted his intentions." The Hawk closed the shutters against the night, refusing to think of Quentin's night in the forest. Would he find the MacLarens? Or would they find him? The man had no lack of courage, to be sure. He frowned, knowing his former Captain of the Guard had not changed in that respect. "He fairly challenged me to cast him into the night, and when I bade him leave in the morning instead, he provoked me."

"How?"

The Hawk spared his wife a smile. "Surely you can guess." She caught her breath. "It was no more than a kiss, because I did cast him out."

"Mhairi must be vexed with you."

"She is." The Hawk sighed.

"He might die in the forest this night," Aileen noted, watching him with care. "Or be killed by the

MacLarens. He might be further maimed, for they are cruel."

"He might, yet I sensed it was the choice he desired of me."

"Why?"

"Perhaps he thinks his life has no merit." The Hawk removed his tabard. "Or perhaps he has a plan to see the MacLarens routed."

"Alone?"

The Hawk smiled a little. "The Quentin I recall had no lack of audacity. He was a clever foe and a bold planner. I would be glad indeed if that talent had not been sacrificed." He nodded, knowing Aileen watched him closely. "You know I must ride to the priory before Sunday."

"We can survive without meat..."

"Game is not what I will hunt," he said, interrupting his wife with resolve. Her eyes widened slightly, but he knew she was not surprised. "You and Nigel will remain here."

"You cannot ride out alone!"

"I will risk no other in this quest. If I am lost, Nigel will become laird, and have your good counsel. Inverfyre will endure. If we three are lost, Inverfyre might fall. I will not surrender easily to that prospect, Aileen. Do not ask me to do as much."

"I hate that they have risen in rebellion again," she said with a savagery he understood.

"As do I, but it must be resolved."

"And you have decided upon your course."

Aileen smiled and shook her head, then offered her hand to him. "I know better than to challenge you when your decision is made," she said. "Though you must know that I will offer any alternatives that occur to me."

The Hawk smiled and kissed her fingertips. "I would expect no less."

"Then come to bed, my lord, and let us savor what is ours this night."

The Hawk gathered his wife into his embrace, intent upon doing exactly that.

CHAPTER FOUR

hey fell upon Quentin like starving dogs.

He was barely out of sight of the gates, a little too far for an archer to strike down a foe, when he heard the rustle of the dead undergrowth on either side. He had that instant of warning before they surrounded him, jumped him, and pummeled him.

Quentin let them take him down easily. He cried out, ensuring his voice was weak, like that of an old man, and dropped immediately to the ground. They beat on him and kicked him and he groaned pitifully, all the while keeping a firm grip upon his walking stick.

Zounds but he was glad of his boiled leather jerkin. He wore the armor hidden beneath his ragged garments and it shielded his body from the worst of the blows. Still, he knew he would be bruised.

If they came close to killing him, they would learn that he was not so meek as he appeared to be, nor so old.

There were five of them by his reckoning, young and strong.

"It is that old cripple," declared one man, perhaps the same who kicked him in the ribs, as if to punctuate the words. "The one who saved the witch."

Someone spat upon him. Quentin was pushed to his back and a fistful of his hair was seized to pull his features into view. He blinked then flinched as a candle was shoved toward his face. He tried to look confused, though his heart skipped at the sight of his opponent.

On the other side of the flame was the ginger-haired man who had fired at Lady Aileen.

Caillen MacLaren.

"Kill him slowly," that man said with a curl of his lip. "Give him time to regret his loyalty to the Hawk."

Quentin cackled like an old woman. He intended to startle them and succeeded. Several stepped back, perhaps fearing he was mad. "Aye, there would be the clever choice. Perhaps there is a good reason the MacLarens are condemned to live in the forest like brute beasts."

"And what reason is that?" Caillen demanded. He was clearly a brash youth, filled with anger and too impetuous to achieve anything of merit. Even if

Quentin had to share some information to gain their trust, this man would not be able to capitalize upon it. The advantages of this rabble were their numbers and their viciousness.

"Your own folly," Quentin said with glee.

Another of the men scowled and punched Quentin in the gut. He curled around the blow as if it had hurt more than it had and coughed weakly. He bit his tongue deliberately while he was hunched over and managed to cough some blood into his spittle.

"So, you think us fools?" Caillen demanded.

"I think it a less than wise choice to kill the one man in your company who knows all about Inverfyre, but then, I am old and some say mad."

That gave them pause.

Caillen leaned down to squint into Quentin's face. Quentin could see that the wound in his shoulder had not been tended well. It was still oozing blood and the blood was cloudy. He could not rely upon the injury to kill the wretch, though. Living in the forest would have made him resilient. "You saved the witch."

"Aye. I hoped to regain the Hawk's favor, but I failed." Quentin let bitterness fill his voice. "He threw me to the wolves years ago. I lost an eye and part of my hand thanks to his *justice*—" he sneered over that word "—but when I came to seek his mercy, when I saved his wife from harm, he hurled me from the gates again. I despise him! Even *she* did not argue my side!" He spat into the dirt and felt the outrage of his audience.

"Bitch," said one.

"They're no better than vermin," said another.

"Where were you all the day?" Caillen demanded.

"In his prison," Quentin lied and tried to look as if he had endured much. "They wanted to know all I knew before flinging me into the night to die."

"And what do you know?" asked a man with a lower voice.

"Nothing!" Quentin wailed. "I saw. I jumped. I risked my own welfare and for this, for this, he would let me die." He dropped his brow to his hand and sobbed.

A wolf howled in the distance and the men glanced over their shoulders, not nearly so brave as they would have him believe.

"I do not believe you," Caillen said and pulled his knife. "We will kill you now and end your misery."

One of the men stayed Caillen with a touch. That he had the power to do as much intrigued Quentin. "Why should we trust you?" he asked quietly and Quentin realized he was the one with the low voice.

"Why should you not?" Quentin whined. "I am injured by the Hawk's choices and left by him to die this night. You have a grievance against him, too, so we have this in common." He raised his hand, letting it shake and ensuring they saw his missing finger. Three of them recoiled. It was the one with the steady gaze, who had the wits amongst them, who did not. His hair was a deep auburn, not unlike Quentin's own. "And I have seen the inside of the keep of Inverfyre. Surely that is of use to you?"

"I have an ally inside the walls already," Caillen said.

"Do you? Has he told you how the Hawk will respond to your attack? Because I know, I know him well, and I have heard enough of his plan to guess the rest." Quentin felt the flicker of their interest. He made a struggle of getting to his feet, relying heavily upon his walking stick. He took a step as if to hobble away and the other men moved to let him pass.

The quiet one, though, stepped into his path. He drew his blade and touched it to Quentin's throat, even as the others closed around him, blocking any escape. "What will he do?"

Quentin shook his head, keeping his voice high and plaintive. "What advantage is there to me in aiding you? I have no guarantee that you will not kill me as soon as I confess what I know."

"You can live until the Hawk rides out, if you share what you know."

Quentin braced his hands upon his walking stick, wavering slightly on his feet. "And after that?"

"It will depend if you are truly loyal to us, or if you prove to be the Hawk's spy."

"If so, you will die slowly!" Caillen said with gusto.

Quentin had no interest in Caillen's threats. He

was a violent fool who would come to a violent end.

His advisor, though, was another matter. That one had cunning.

Quentin would use it against him.

He nodded once. "He will leave the matter a day or maybe two to lull you into believing that he has let the insult pass. Not much more than that, though, for he has an errand to perform."

"An errand?"

"Sunday is the first Sunday of Advent," Quentin reminded them but was rewarded only with blank stares. "He must fetch the *Titulus Croce* from the priory," he said. "He must show it at the Mass, to prove his right to be laird."

The quiet one nodded and smiled. "And he will ride out with an army to fetch it."

Quentin shook his head. "Neither his lady nor his heir will leave Inverfyre. He will not put them at risk."

"He will ride alone?" Caillen laughed. "We shall take him easily."

Quentin spared that one a glance, a glance that the advisor noted.

"What would you counsel?" that man asked, his blade still cold against Quentin's throat.

"I would let him ride as far and as wide as he chooses, and remain out of his path. Let him mark the entire perimeter of Inverfyre and find naught at all. Let him be reassured that all is well, for then he will retrieve his prize."

"Who will ride with him?" asked the quiet one.

"At least one of his most loyal warriors will ride with him, to see to his own safety. Perhaps several archers."

That man nodded and turned to survey the road. "And there is a length of road between keep and priory that is out of range of the archers. I like the notion of them watching from the walls as their laird is robbed and killed, yet unable to come to his aid in time."

"An eye for an eye," Quentin said, touching his own eye patch.

"Dubhglas MacLaren lost an eye, thanks to the kin of the Hawk," Caillen said with gusto, at least having the wits to understand the reference. "I will claim the Hawk's eye in my cousin's memory!"

The advisor smiled. "And when we capture the holy relic, the *Titulus Croce*, we will hold the mark of legitimacy of every Laird of Inverfyre, brought to this holding by Magnus Armstrong."

Quentin nodded. "Take the *Titulus* and it could be argued before the king that you are the rightful Laird of Inverfyre."

"But I care naught for the king!" Caillen protested.

Quentin hid his impatience with this notion. How could any man aspire to be a laird yet think he could then ignore the king? He kept silent, though, aware that the quiet rebel watched him closely.

Caillen gestured to the keep that the Hawk had built, with its high walls and enclosed village. "The king, if he had a measure of sense, would have declared this entire structure to be an intrusion upon our ancestral land. I have no respect for the law, for it can be bought with coin." Caillen's eyes shone with malice as he leaned closer to Quentin. "But I will exact my own justice. I will kill every soul who swears fealty to the Hawk, cutting them down with my own blade."

"Aye," murmured his violent allies, the bloodlust thrumming in their voices.

Quentin felt that he was in the presence of wickedness but he did not protest. "Might can oft make right," he contented himself with saying.

Caillen continued with enthusiasm. "Aye! Inverfyre will be stained red with the blood of the traitors who pledge to the Hawk when I make it mine own."

"Aye," said the quiet one. "And when the keep is claimed, you should marry his pretty daughter Evangeline, with force, if need be."

Caillen responded to the suggestion merrily. "Aye, Faolan! There is a fine notion. She will welcome me to her bed to stop the carnage, and I will ride her so often that the hall will be filled with our sons. We shall live in triumph at Inverfyre!" The rabble cheered this notion with gusto.

"And who is your trusted advisor?" Quentin asked when the din quieted.

"My own brother, the sole one I can trust," Caillen said.

Once it was said, Quentin saw the resemblance between them.

"For the other, Ramsay, is as like to ally with the Hawk as with us," said Faolan and spat at the ground.

Three brothers then, and only two rebelling against the Hawk.

Quentin wagered that Caillen was oldest, which was why he had claimed leadership. He seemed also to have a measure of charisma, which compensated for his lack of wit. Perhaps it was his violence that drew the others to him, but Quentin saw their loyalty shining in their eyes.

Caillen gave Quentin a shove. "Give me your pledge, old man, that you will aid us to defeat the Hawk. Otherwise, you will be the first of his allies to taste my blade."

It was a ridiculous proposition, for there was only one thing he could say.

"I told you already that I would be of aid to you," he whined. "I told you already what the Hawk would do. If you are so faithless as to slaughter me now in return for my goodwill, then you are no better than he." He fumbled at the neck of his chemise, baring the skin of his throat to view, ensuring that his hand trembled. He addressed Faolan, who yet held the knife, for he guessed that man would make the choice. "Strike here and kill me though I am unarmed, and see the deed done quickly."

Their gazes locked and held, but Quentin heard the murmur of dissent amongst Caillen's followers. They were not inclined to mercy, to be sure, but his comment about faithlessness troubled them.

"I say we let the old man live," Faolan said with quiet force, sheathing his blade before Caillen replied. "He might yet be useful to us."

Caillen nodded reluctant assent, proving again that it was Faolan who held the power. "You can live, old man, thanks to my brother's plea. I suggest you prove your measure, for when the Hawk rides out, your fate will be decided."

"I would beg for shelter and food."

"And you will be disappointed," Caillen scoffed. "You will not sleep with us."

"Then where?"

"Wherever you like." Faolan gestured to the forest. He then leaned closer and lowered his voice. His gaze was hard, his manner chilling. "But do not try to run, old man. We will find you. If you try to flee or betray us, we will bind you and ensure you suffer so that death is welcome. I know these woods. There is no corner in which you can hide."

Quentin dropped his gaze as if frightened and let himself tremble. "You know this forest?" he echoed. "But it is so vast!"

Faolan smiled. "We were aware of you as soon as you stepped over the borders of Inverfyre," he said softly. "We let you hear our plan, in order to learn your intention."

Quentin looked up, not needing to feign surprise, and Faolan' gaze was unswerving.

"We do not care about the Lady of Inverfyre. We wanted to draw out the Hawk from his fortress.

That you saved her means that he will ride out in search of vengeance. He will not return to his lady's bed alive." His smile broadened. "So, you proved your usefulness in that, which is why I say you can live another night."

Quentin was chilled. He had been used and not realized as much.

Truly, he had lost his skills as surely as he had lost his finger.

The revelation only buttressed his desire to see Inverfyre rid of these brothers and their followers.

The young rebels smiled, so smug in their surety that all would proceed their way that another man might have been tempted to injure them immediately. Quentin shivered and groveled as if afraid, begging for their tolerance. He even fell to the ground and kissed Caillen's rough boot, as if desperate to ingratiate himself, until Caillen shook him off with a laugh.

"Go then, old man. Know that you will be watched until the Hawk is dead."

Caillen strode away then, his cohorts snickering before they followed him. Only Faolan glanced back, giving Quentin a level look that was a warning.

Quentin did not imagine that he was unobserved, even when he could no longer see Caillen's party. He kept his figure bent and shuffled deeper into the forest, thinking furiously. This Faolan was the brother with the wits and doubtless the ambition. If Caillen were killed, Faolan would assume the leadership of the rebels.

It was clear to Quentin that Caillen had been used as well. He would be blamed for the assault on Lady Aileen and the Hawk would seek retribution from him, believing Caillen to be the leader. It was Faolan who must die, for it was Faolan who schemed for the MacLarens. He ceded to Caillen for the moment, but Quentin did not doubt that he meant to let the Hawk remove Caillen and be blamed for the death of another of the men in the forest. If both brothers died, Quentin would wager that the other rebels would scatter for lack of leadership.

Did the Hawk know about Faolan? Perhaps not, though that brother was the greater foe.

Quentin would see him dead, if it was his own last living deed. Mhairi could never be safe so long as Faolan drew breath.

Indeed, he looked forward to completing that task.

Mhairi dreamed.

She was in the forest beyond Inverfyre's walls, in the shelter that had been built by the old wise woman, Adaira, though it did not look precisely as she recalled. The walls were more solid than she knew them to be, for the silver trees that formed the walls had grown so tightly together that there was scarcely a chink between them. They glowed against the darkness of the night, like pounded silver, and the fire on the hearth seemed to pulse red light.

She was dressed in her best kirtle, as if she would attend a celebration. It was the deep blue one that had been made for her the year before, the one with golden embroidery thick on the hem and the cuffs of the sleeves. She wore a veil of sheerest gold cloth, an indulgence from Ravensmuir's stores, and a gemmed circlet perched on her brow.

She went to the portal and looked into the shadows of the forest, impatient to depart the comfort of the hut. She felt an imperative to leave, though she could not explain it.

Mhairi shivered in her sleep at her own impulse, for she knew the forest was full of predators.

But in her dream, she abandoned the hut with confidence, picking up her skirts as she walked. The snow was falling fast and thick. It covered the ground with fearsome speed, blanketing all with endless white. As it snowed, the forest was cast into unnatural quiet. Not a breath of wind stirred.

Indeed, the only movement in the forest was that of Mhairi.

She should have had her crossbow and Freya on her fist in the forest, but she was unarmed. She might have been at Kinfairlie instead of Inverfyre and Mhairi stirred in her sleep, knowing her confidence in her safety was undeserved.

Despite that, she strode through the snow, which was already past her knees. She was not cold, even though she had no cloak on this night of nights. The keep of Inverfyre rose behind her, more of a presence than a visible landmark given the weather, but Mhairi moved steadily away from it.

She had not been cast out like Quentin, but she had chosen to leave. She would follow her desire and her love, and seek him out.

To match her fate to his.

It was folly. It was madness. She should have dressed to survive and brought provisions, but in her dream, she was untroubled by the implications of her choices.

A wolf howled but she ignored it as if it were no more important than a fish in the river.

She saw the light ahead, a strange blue glow, and her heart skipped with anticipation. There. Quentin would be there. Mhairi set her course toward the light without hesitation. Indeed, she began to run as she drew near and heard the music.

Fey music.

Fey laughter.

She raced into the clearing from which the light emanated, without halting to study her surroundings beforehand, which was proof enough that this vision was unreal.

More evidence came from the clearing itself. She spun in place to see every detail, her heart filled with joy. The clearing could have been a great hall, made entirely of ice. The high arching walls glittered. Snowflakes danced within its bounds and the music soared. The ceiling looked like the midnight sky crowded with stars, although the sky beyond the bounds of this magical clearing was overcast.

But the splendor was not the source of Mhairi's delight. Nay, there was one person in the clearing.

A man.

A knight.

He was dressed in silver and indigo, his cape trimmed with ermine, his tabard embroidered with silver snowflakes that glistened as if they were made of frost. He turned and smiled at her, tall and straight and true, and Mhairi's heart clenched so tightly that she nigh stumbled.

Quentin.

Healed.

Indeed, the heat in his gaze made her breath catch. Though she could see no musicians, the music changed to a familiar tune, one to which they danced at Inverfyre each Yule. Quentin offered his hand to her.

There was no man of greater honor, no warrior more true.

Mhairi stepped toward him with pleasure, her chin high. She put her hand in his and felt the welcome strength and heat of his fingers close over hers, then he spun her in the dance. She laughed as they matched their steps, as she remembered dancing thus when she had been a child, as they danced with increasing speed and joy. His gaze never strayed from her, his lips curved in a proud smile, and she felt like a treasured beauty.

They were together.

The music lilted to a close, and Quentin drew her into his embrace. "Be mine," he murmured for her ears alone and Mhairi nodded ready agreement.

"Only yours," she agreed and saw the flicker of pleasure in his eyes.

"Forever allied," he murmured, then bent to capture her lips beneath his own once more. Heat surged through Mhairi, heat and satisfaction, and happiness for their shared future.

Mhairi awakened suddenly, shivering with cold, and realized there was snow drifting through the shutters of the chamber she shared with her sister. Evangeline was curled up in a bundle upon her pallet, apparently having claimed all the pelts for herself.

It had only been a dream.

And she had no shared future with Quentin.

At least not as yet.

Mhairi left her pallet to fetch her cloak, the one lined with rabbit fur which she had not worn in her dream. She went to the window to see if she could fasten the shutter more securely and looked out into the forest, now covered in snow.

It was quiet and still, blanketed in white.

Quentin was out there.

The MacLarens were out there.

She bit her lip in fear for him.

Forever allied. She recalled that light of triumph and her sense that he was less injured than he appeared to be.

Do you trust me?

Had he kissed her in the hall to provoke the Hawk into casting him out?

If so, then Quentin had a plan. He was not a fool who failed to understand the peril of the forest in winter, especially when there were traitors abroad. She nodded to herself. He must intend to gain the trust of the MacLarens, but it was not because he had turned against her father. Quentin's word was true and he had pledged fealty to her father more than a decade before.

He meant to foil the MacLarens' scheme, whatever it was.

It had been Quentin who had taught her that opposition was not always the best strategy, that sometimes it was easier to use preconceptions against a foe.

He had said he was not trusted at Inverfyre, so he meant to use that distrust to gain credibility with the MacLarens. He had needed the Hawk to spurn him to give credence to the notion of him being an enemy of her father.

He risked much in this, but that was characteristic of the Quentin she knew and loved.

Mhairi had to help.

Quentin still had a blind side, so long as he wore the eye patch. She would defend it, and prove to him that they were stronger together than apart.

She would prove to her father that she and Quentin should truly be allied forever.

The night was already cold. Quentin went some distance before he found a place where the trees seemed to grow around each other, enclosing a space the size of a hut. He ran his hand over the entwined boughs, unable to escape the sense that they created a living refuge. Did he feel a pulse beneath his palm when he laid it against the tree? Surely that was whimsy.

It seemed clear to him that the trees had been bent deliberately as they grew, and he wondered by whom. It would have taken years to shape this shelter. He stepped through the single opening and felt a sense of tranquility flood through himself and no longer cared who had created this space.

It was a haven.

And there was a small hearth made of river stones. The smoke would reveal his location, but they watched him at any rate and the heat would be more than welcome.

Quentin gathered some wood, his decision made. He would sleep here.

It was only after he had kindled a small blaze and huddled near it, wrapped in his cloak, that a vision unfolded in his thoughts. It was a waking dream.

It made his heart soar, for in his dream, he danced with Mhairi.

And he was whole, as he would never be again.

The Hawk awakened alone in the great bed in the solar, which was uncommon. It was still early, but Aileen stood at the window, looking over the forest.

It had snowed during the night.

He recognized her posture and cleared his throat before he spoke. "You dreamed?"

"Of my mother," Aileen acknowledged. "She showed me the hazel and the honeysuckle again."

"Are you with child?" the Hawk asked, for the same dream had been the first tidings of such happy news in the past. The possibility troubled him, not because he would not welcome another in their family but because he would fear for Aileen.

She glanced over her shoulder and smiled. "Nay and I am glad of that. Childbirth is for the young."

"Then what?" He rose and donned a cloak, going to her side. The wind was crisp this morning and the forests of Inverfyre looked peaceful, though he knew they were not. His banner snapped above the tower of the priory and he hoped Quentin was well.

"The honeysuckle and the hazel," she murmured, placing her hand over his. "One of our children has found her partner."

The Hawk bristled. He disliked portentous dreams and omens, and disliked even more his sense that he knew who his wife meant.

"Mhairi is named for my mother," Aileen reminded him gently.

"She is too young."

"She will always be too young for you to want to surrender her hand to Quentin."

The Hawk winced and went to wash. He did not want to argue with Aileen or with Mhairi.

"What if her instincts are better than yours?" Aileen asked quietly. "What if she is right about his merit?" She turned to face him and the Hawk glanced up. "What if you aided the attainment of her goal instead of obstructing it?"

He had no answer. He did not know sufficient to make a choice.

But as the Hawk descended to the hall, he reconsidered Quentin's words and his choices, and he wondered.

CHAPTER FIVE

hairi rose early on the morning after her dream. Evangeline still slept, her head buried beneath the pelts, and their maid had yet to come to them. Mhairi washed in cold water and unfolded the blue kirtle from her trunk. She dressed quickly, wanting to be out of the chamber before Evangeline awakened and began to ask questions. She was still securing the end of her plait when she darted down the stairs.

As she had anticipated, the hall was still quiet.

But there was a rumble of voices from the chamber where her father kept his accounts. She hurried toward the closed door, recognizing the voices of her father and of his old comrade Ahearn O'Donnell.

Mhairi was relieved. She liked Ahearn better than Reinhard.

She rapped on the door to announce her presence and there was immediate silence. Ahearn opened the door, his brows rising at the sight of her. "Good morning," he said quietly then glanced over his shoulder to the Hawk.

"Come to chastise me?" her father asked with characteristic calm. His gaze swept over her kirtle. "Or do you mean to charm me instead?"

"I offered the kiss."

"I do not doubt it." Her father shook his head. "He took what he had no right to take, just as he taught you what he had no right to teach you. I will not suffer a man in my hall who cannot be relied upon, even if his crippled state demands pity."

"He is not crippled," Mhairi said and felt the surprise of both men.

The Hawk leaned back against the table, his arms folded across his chest. "He limps. He has lost one eye and one finger. He is feeble."

"I believe it is all feigned, save the lost finger and perhaps the eye." She stepped forward as her father and his comrade exchanged a glance. "I believe he came to keep his word to me, but I also believe he doubted you would welcome him. He told me long ago that it was best to be seen as less of a threat when encountering a foe."

Ahearn cleared his throat. "I recall the same counsel from him."

"Reinhard was not convinced of his good intentions," the Hawk noted.

"It would be easier to change the course of the

93

sun than to change Reinhard's assessment in any matter," Ahearn said with a smile.

"And so Quentin used Reinhard's attitude instead of trying to change it. He asked if I trusted him, then requested a kiss," Mhairi said.

Her father's gaze was steady. "He provoked my reaction. I thought as much at the time."

"To approach the MacLarens as an ally and defeat them from within!" Mhairi concluded.

"What are you thinking?" the Hawk asked.

"He was always a brilliant strategist, adept at defying expectations," Ahearn said. "I recall also that he had pledged fealty to you until death. Perhaps Mhairi is right."

The Hawk frowned. "I had forgotten how he changed his vows."

"And so what if he *is* loyal to you yet, Papa?" Mhairi dared to ask.

"It would be like him to plan thus," Ahearn mused. "I recall a strategy suggested once by Quentin," Ahearn said. "When we had to spirit the treasury from Abernye."

Mhairi held her breath. She had been very young when her grandfather's holding had been attacked and her father had ridden to the rescue. She recalled that Quentin had been new to Inverfyre and had shown himself well.

The Hawk rubbed his chin. "The scheme that saw me make him Captain of the Guard. It was clever and fooled the foes of my wife's father. We lost only one man and slaughtered eight of them, then easily captured the rest."

Ahearn raised a finger. "And he said then that we would not have lost that knight, if we had possessed a single ally outside the walls."

The Hawk spun to face Mhairi. "What makes you suspect that he is not so injured as he appears?"

Mhairi knew better than to cite the evidence of a dream to her father. "He walked more quickly and stood taller when he crossed the hall to me."

Ahearn smiled. "I would wager it was immediately after his plan was made. I accused him once of that sign of his decisiveness being his sole weakness."

The Hawk was watching Mhairi. "I think Quentin's sole weakness stands before me, dressed to make an appeal on his behalf."

Mhairi felt herself flush but she did not look away. "You must know that I begged him to teach me the arts of war all those years ago, and how to throw a knife." And more, but Mhairi did not confess that.

"And you must know that if my warning to him had no power, then it was dangerous for him to remain in my hall."

Mhairi nodded reluctant agreement, because she knew her father waited for it.

As soon as she had done so, the Hawk gestured to the door. "I thank you for your insight, Mhairi, and appreciate your defense of Quentin, but now would have you leave."

"But I would be of aid!"

"You will do no such deed!" Her father's eyes blazed. Your place is within these walls until the MacLarens are defeated."

Mhairi did not nod and she did not agree. She hoped her father did not notice the omission. She curtseyed to him and left his chamber, closing the door behind herself.

Then she leaned her ear against the crack to listen.

"What if we use that same strategy again?" she heard her father ask Ahearn. "If Quentin has won the trust of the MacLarens, then he will recognize it. He might be able to aid us."

"I think it a wise course," Ahearn said. "We have to retrieve the *Titulus* from the priory by Sunday."

"And I will not surrender the errand to any other man. They will know that."

"I will ride with you," Ahearn said.

"I welcome you by my side. I will see this resolved at midday." The Hawk listed the men who would be in his party and tersely outlined his strategy.

Quentin's strategy.

His voice dropped low so the words were difficult to discern, but Mhairi had heard enough to recognize the trap and how it was baited.

Aye, Quentin had explained it to her once, when teaching her of the defense of a holding surrounded by enemies.

She knew exactly how she could participate, though she must ensure that no one guessed the truth before her father rode out.

After all, Quentin had oft said that surprise was the most potent weapon in any warrior's arsenal and the MacLarens would not be expecting her.

☙❧

Quentin awakened to the sound of a hunting horn. Whoever blew upon it gave a lengthy salute and the sound echoed off the hills, a fair warning that the Laird of Inverfyre would ride out this very day.

He scrambled to his feet in the hut of silvery trees, shook the snow out of his cloak, and seized his walking stick. He limped toward the road, and quickly spied the MacLarens gathering in the forest. He could see the line of silver trees along the road and to the left, the high walls of the newer keep of Inverfyre. To the right was the rebuilt fortress of Inverfyre, which was currently the priory.

"And now we learn if you are correct, old man," Caillen said, his tone taunting.

His brother simply surveyed Quentin and said nothing at all. Had he walked too quickly? Did Faolan have suspicions?

"He will assert his authority by riding between the two keeps first," Quentin said, hoping it would be so.

The rebels nodded. Quentin could see three dozen of them, mostly young men, all in rags and thinner than would be ideal. Their expressions were tinged with envy, hatred and resentment, and they gripped knives and swords of mixed value.

Stolen, probably.

Sharpened, undoubtedly.

The gates opened at Inverfyre and the portcullis groaned as it was raised. The horn was blown again and the Hawk appeared, riding his black destrier. The stallion snorted and stomped, proudly tossing his head, and fairly danced in his impatience to run. The sight reminded Quentin all too well of Tyr and he swallowed, putting the memory aside in this moment.

"Who is with him?" Caillen demanded in a whisper.

Another rebel leaned toward the road. "Does he ride out alone?"

Faolan reached out and snatched the collar of that man, hauling him forcibly back into the shadows. "Do not make the mistake of being seen," he hissed.

Another warrior appeared to the left of the Hawk and Quentin recognized Reinhard, as much by his figure as his colors. His destrier was no less magnificent, though this horse had white socks.

Faolan gave Quentin a look. "Reinhard, Captain of the Guard."

Quentin nodded agreement. It was no coincidence that Reinhard took that flank, for he was adept with a blade in his left hand while the Hawk favored his right.

Three more men fell in behind the pair, two riding alongside each other and one in the rear. The last was Ahearn, Quentin thought, who had a rare talent for fighting from the saddle, regardless of which hand he used. The middle pair of warriors carried loaded crossbows, and all wore chain mail and helmets. They carried long shields on their outside arms, and their horses wore caparisons of chain mail. By remaining in a tight cluster, they were armored on all sides.

Quentin doubted it was a coincidence that they rode just as he had directed the Hawk's men to ride at the siege of Abernye. Had Mhairi convinced the Hawk to trust Quentin after all? Only the unfolding of the strategy would prove the truth.

He glanced into the forest. The snow made it easier to see the MacLarens, even when they perched in the trees or tried to hide in the undergrowth. The boughs were barren and the lighting stark. In a way, they had chosen the timing of their assault badly, for summer's greenery would have hidden them better.

The gates closed behind the Hawk. The walls of Inverfyre bristled with guards. The walls of the priory were similarly defended. The sun burst from the clouds as the Hawk commenced his ride, the breath of his destrier white in the air, and the sunlight glinted off helms and blades.

Five in the Hawk's party.

Several dozen in the forest.

Quentin did not like the odds. He hoped with all his heart that the Hawk employed the rest of that strategy from Abernye.

A woman appeared at the summit of Inverfyre's defending walls and Quentin recognized Lady Aileen. The dark-haired man in armor beside her had to be Nigel. "Hail the Laird of Inverfyre!" she cried and raised her fist to the sky. Quentin was startled to see a white gyrfalcon launch from Lady Aileen's fist.

The bird's massive wings beat so slowly that it seemed it should fall out of the sky, but it soared high, almost disappearing into the blue overhead. It was the perfect distraction and that was the moment that Quentin was certain of the Hawk's intention. All gazes followed the bird's course as it flew to the priory, then back toward the Hawk's keep. He lifted his fist and the bird descended to him with speed and power.

Just before it landed upon his outstretched fist, one of the MacLarens hurled a rock at the bird. "Death to the Laird of Inverfyre!" he shouted.

"Hoy!" the Hawk cried, but the raptor had already seen the projectile. With a scream of outrage, it flew out of range. The MacLarens all watched bird and laird, which was their first mistake. One of the Hawk's archers had already loosed a bolt and it landed in the chest of the man who had cast the stone. He staggered backward from the force of impact, blood streaming from the wound, and a second bolt buried itself in his forehead.

He fell bleeding in the snow and moved no more.

"Leave him," Faolan whispered when the others would have surged forward. "It is too late to aid him."

There was a coolness in his tone that told Quentin the gesture had been planned.

As was the sacrifice of this man's life.

Why would Faolan have put the Hawk on his guard, instead of letting him pass unchallenged?

"You are curious," that man murmured from beside Quentin, even as the Hawk approached the gates of the priory. "It would have been odd for us to fail to take one chance," he continued. "Silence would have fed the Hawk's suspicion more than this."

Quentin doubted that the Hawk believed his adversaries to be cowed, but he merely nodded, as if Faolan were beyond wise.

The passing party began to gallop, the horses' hooves making a thunderous noise. Quentin listened with care but could not discern the sound of the trap being set. Was he wrong?

When the Hawk passed beneath the gates of the priory, a cheer erupted from the garrison. He turned and immediately rode back to the keep with his party, his destrier galloping and the party separating slightly. Faolan smiled beside Quentin, nodding that his feint had apparently worked. This time, the MacLarens remained silent and hidden.

The Hawk rode the boundary of his immediate holding then. Quentin heard his party gallop down the road toward Aberfinnan, following the River

Fyre to its junction with the mightier Finnan. It was not long before another celebratory hoot from the men at the keep revealed that the Hawk was safely returned.

Then he appeared again on the road to the priory. Quentin clenched the head of his walking stick as the Hawk's party passed once more without challenge. The sun was high now and the gyrfalcon was circling, its white form bright against the blue sky. His heart was in his throat when the Hawk's party disappeared into the priory, for he knew what they had collected there.

"And now he fetches the prize," Faolan whispered.

Quentin nodded, still unable to hear the warriors that he believed were behind him in the forest, surrounding the MacLarens. He prayed he was not mistaken.

The Hawk's party left the priory, assembled in their formation again. A sixth had joined their party, riding between the two archers and carrying a chest in his lap.

Faolan straightened at the sight and Caillen grinned. The younger brother put his hand on the shoulder of the older.

"*Wait,*" he mouthed, though Caillen was as anxious to spring forth as a hound that has caught a scent.

The moments stretched long. The horses seemed to move as if in slow motion and Quentin's heart thundered.

The Hawk rode into the zone that was out of range of the archers at either priory or keep. The party drew alongside the hiding place of the MacLarens, and Reinhard glanced down at the dead rebel beside the road.

"Go," Faolan murmured and two young boys raced out of the forest. They flung themselves at the Hawk's party, and struck the horses with the rocks in their hands. The stallions whinnied and shied, the formation breaking apart with precision. It only looked like chaos. Quentin knew it was planned. The archers raising their bows even as the Hawk shouted.

"They are but children!" he roared and the archers hesitated.

Which was what Faolan was relying upon.

The MacLarens burst from the forest like a swarm of rats, taking advantage of that hesitation. They hurled themselves into the horses, beating and scratching upon them, driving their bodies between the riders. Some even flung snow into the faces of the knights and horses. From the forest, a volley of arrows were launched, their fleches quivering as their heads buried themselves in the flesh of both men and horse. None of the injuries were critical in themselves, but the confusion appeared to put the Hawk in peril.

The Hawk drew his sword with a roar and the bloodshed began. Some MacLarens were struck down and others stumbled, only to be stepped upon by the horses. The gyrfalcon circled, screaming.

But the Hawk's party seemed to be broken by the assault. Reinhard's steed was the first to bolt. The stallion reared and whinnied, then raced for the priory. Two palfreys followed the stallion's lead, even though their riders continued to shoot arrows into the mob of MacLarens. Ahearn cursed as his destrier appeared to take the bit in its teeth and race back to the keep alone. The rider with the trunk cried out as his palfrey dove into the forest on the far side of the road. A dozen MacLarens raced after him at Faolan's gesture, hooting as they pursued horse and prize.

The Hawk was left alone.

The ploy was perfectly executed, just as Quentin had once planned at the board at Abernye.

And the MacLarens believed it.

The MacLarens encircled the Hawk, their ranks two-deep, but stayed out of range of his sword. He circled the horse in place until Caillen stepped out of the forest. Then he turned to face the supposed leader, an armored knight on his destrier, facing down a ruffian dressed in rags.

"What do you want, spawn of the MacLarens?" the Hawk demanded, as if he were in charge of the situation. Indeed, he was, though his foes did not know it as yet. Quentin was aware that both Reinhard and Ahearn had not entered the gates of their destinations and guessed that they circled around with the other warriors to close the trap.

"You will make me laird," Caillen said.

"Will I?" the Hawk asked, his amusement at the

notion most clear. "You have miscalculated, Caillen MacLaren," he said, then touched his heels to his destrier's side and charged toward Caillen, his sword swinging high.

Faolan moved in that very moment, lifting his bow and drawing back the arrow. He aimed for the Hawk's face but in the very instant that he would have loosed the bow, Quentin leaped upon him. He ripped the bow from the rebel's hands and punched him in the face. The arrow shot wide of its mark, soaring over the head of the Hawk and the rebels shouted with frustration.

Faolan struck Quentin in the face, then kicked him, writhing free of Quentin's grip when the others assaulted him. He was pounded once again, but did not care. He let them beat him and tried to keep track of Faolan. That man fled into the forest, abandoning his kin, and ducking into the shadows.

The Hawk sliced down Caillen with a single blow, which sent alarm through the ranks of the rebels. They turned to flee just as the Hawk's warriors were revealed in the forest behind them. Those men had crept from both keep and priory as the Hawk made his ceremonial ride, the beat of the horses' hooves upon the road disguising the sound of their movements. Ahearn and Reinhard shouted from opposite directions, then lunged into the fray on their steeds. The Hawk's forces fell upon the surprised MacLarens with force, disarming them and capturing them, and leaving no small number of them dead. The fight was short and vicious, its outcome beyond doubt.

Until Faolan whistled from the road. Quentin's heart stopped when he saw that the more cunning of the brothers had a small company behind him. One carried the trunk for the *Titulus*. A second held a knife at the throat of the rider who had been entrusted with that burden. The palfrey was also behind the band.

And Faolan himself held the braid of a second captive, his satisfaction clear.

Mhairi, garbed as a boy with fury in her eyes.

The Hawk was impassive, though Quentin could feel that man's outrage.

"Perhaps you will make me Laird of Inverfyre," Faolan taunted. "Or perhaps I should ride to the king and ask him to bestow the honor."

Quentin assessed the distance even as he considered the merit of the bow he had claimed from Faolan. It was not as fine a weapon as he would have liked for a shot of such importance.

He could have made the shot with certainty—if Mhairi did not move, if he had yet possessed both eyes, if the bow had been better crafted. He yearned in that moment for his old faith in his abilities, the faith that had been stolen from him along with everything else.

He could not risk failure, not when Mhairi would pay the price.

The Hawk urged his destrier to take a step closer to Faolan. "What makes you believe I would wager with the likes of you?" he demanded.

"Your daughter's life!" Faolan cried. He pulled Mhairi in front of himself, evidently trying to keep himself from being a target, and lifted a knife to her throat.

Quentin knew the moment that Mhairi saw him. Her gaze did not linger, lest she reveal him, but he felt it as surely as a touch. He remembered asking if she trusted him. He recalled the words in his dream that they would be allies forever.

She would give him the opportunity.

All he needed was the courage to take it, to believe in his skills, to trust in his instincts.

Just as he had instructed her, all those years before.

Quentin loaded the bow and raised it in one fluid gesture. In that same moment, Mhairi stamped on Faolan's foot and drove her elbow into his side. His blade nicked her throat, but she ducked quickly, leaving him in view. The Hawk bellowed and touched his heels to his destrier's flanks, but the shot was not his to take.

Quentin released the arrow, trusting in his aim.

Then he watched as it sliced through the air. It landed, quivering, in Faolan's throat. The rebel's blood began to flow from the wound but he roared all the same, then he tried to snatch at Mhairi. She twisted from his desperate grip, pulled Quentin's own dagger from its hiding place beneath her tabard, and drove it into his poor excuse for a heart.

Faolan fell before the Hawk could reach him, tumbling to his knees in shock, wavering there, then falling into the dirt. It was Mhairi who kicked his corpse to retrieve her knife, wiping the blood on his ragged garments before she spat upon him with disgust. Then she stood tall to greet her father, who swept her into the saddle before himself, clearly both shaken and relieved.

Quentin smiled. His warrior maiden had not only learned her lessons well but had reminded him that he was not so useless as he had feared.

Perhaps he had a future, after all.

Quentin had proven himself!

Mhairi was triumphant. She did not care what her father said to her now. Even the Hawk could not deny that Quentin had saved him from injury and her, as well. Quentin's skills were as good as ever, his aim was perfect, and his instincts unassailable. They had not lost a single man—because they had possessed an ally in the forest. She could scarce wait for the moment when her father acknowledged Quentin and granted his due.

In the meantime, there were prisoners to be secured and corpses to be gathered. The trunk seized by Faolan proved to hold nothing more valuable than a stone, just as Mhairi had anticipated. The company returned to the priory in a merry mood. The minor injuries they had sustained were treated and the mood was celebratory.

Soon enough, they returned to Inverfyre with the *Titulus Croce*, Skuld flying overhead. Quentin was offered a palfrey and climbed into the saddle, his gaze sliding past Mhairi.

At his command, she rode beside her father.

"You defied me," he said when they were on the road and no others could hear them.

"I made no promise," she said and a smile touched his lips.

"I noticed that at the time and wondered at its import. You could have been killed, Mhairi, and I would have been heartsick." He frowned. "Your mother would have been devastated."

"I had to help. I had to see."

"So you hid in the company that crept from Inverfyre when I was riding to the priory."

She nodded, not surprised that he had guessed.

"And you followed the trunk for the *Titulus*."

"I thought to retrieve it for you. I was sure that I could fight a few boys with success."

"Yet you did not."

Mhairi smiled. "I chose to be captured, Papa, for then I knew they would return to taunt you with their apparent success. It was the easiest means of ensuring that the *Titulus* did not disappear into the forest."

"A clever strategy." The Hawk granted her a considering glance, but his tone was benign. "I suppose you intend to remind me that you had a good teacher."

Mhairi smiled. "I do not think I need to."

"You did not know that the key to his own strategy was to let the villains capture the prize and believe they had won. You took an unnecessary risk."

"I do not regret it."

"And I am not surprised. You are your mother's daughter, to be sure." Before Mhairi could reply, the Hawk beckoned to Quentin, who urged his horse to walk alongside the Hawk's destrier. "You have come to my aid twice on this day, by saving me from harm and also by executing that MacLaren."

"Faolan MacLaren, my lord," Quentin supplied. "The younger brother of Caillen."

"Then we are well rid of them both. You knew of him earlier?"

"Not until I left Inverfyre last night and they attacked me. It quickly became clear that he was the more cunning of the pair."

"And I would have been satisfied with Caillen's death alone, without your aid. I thank you for this service, Quentin."

Quentin bowed. "I am honored to have done it, my lord."

"Did you learn anything else of merit from them?"

"They said they had a third brother, one Ramsay, who they believed more likely to ally with you than to challenge you."

The Hawk smiled a little. "A MacLaren? I think they called that matter wrong. But the fact remains that I am in your debt—yet I would put myself in it further."

"Sir?"

"Will you deliver a missive for me? I should like to send some tidings to my niece and her husband at Killairig before the Yule. You may take a horse, of course, and some provisions. It will not take you ten days to reach their abode, independent of the weather."

Mhairi frowned in confusion. What tidings would her father send to Annelise and Garrett? And why would he send Quentin from Inverfyre again, without respite?

"Aye, sir. I will be honored to render this service," Quentin said, though Mhairi heard a coolness in his tone.

Was it unreasonable that he might hope for more than an errand from her father?

And why was her father sending Quentin away again?

❧

Mhairi knew it was no accident that she had no opportunity to speak with Quentin that night, or that Evangeline was intent upon keeping her in their chamber that night.

She dreamed of the clearing again that night, and danced with Quentin there. In her dream, she felt a joy that abandoned her at first light.

She awakened to the sounds of horses being saddled but found the chamber door locked. She stood at the window and watched as Quentin mounted the palfrey and rode down to the gates of Inverfyre.

He did not look back. The set of his shoulders told her all she needed to know.

Quentin would not return.

CHAPTER SIX

reparations for Christmas were embraced at Inverfyre with merriment. It seemed a sweeter Yuletide since the MacLarens were routed and the forests were safe. Laird and lady had ridden to hunt in the weeks since the triumph and there was venison aplenty for all. The hall was hung with greens and the Yule log already blazed on the hearth.

Mhairi, though, could not find her customary pleasure in the season. Each Sunday at the Mass, she kissed the *Titulus* and prayed that Quentin was well.

She feared she would never see him again.

She was certain she would never forget him.

It was four days before the Yule itself when a trio of horses arrived unexpectedly at Inverfyre's gates. Like the others drawn by the sound of hoofbeats, Mhairi left the bailey for the village.

Three horses of Ravensmuir's breeding, as black as midnight, pranced through the gates, nostrils flared and flanks gleaming from their run. Their necks arched proudly, and their manes flowed long.

Her cousin, Malcolm Lammergeier, the Laird of Ravensmuir, led the group, his stallion the darkest of them all. His companion rode a dark mare, only slightly smaller than Malcolm's stallion. Malcolm led a third stallion, almost as tall as his own. The horse's mane had been cropped shorter, as was his tail, but his breeding was evident. There was a tiny white star upon his brow and Mhairi caught her breath in recognition.

It was Quentin's destrier!

"Is it Tyr?" she asked when Malcolm halted before her, unwilling to even delay her question by greeting him.

Malcolm laughed. "I believe it is, but would have someone identify him here."

"Tyr!" the Hawk exclaimed as he joined them. Malcolm winked at Mhairi as her father and the ostler ran their hands over the stallion. Tyr nuzzled the ostler and nibbled his hair, then exhaled and stamped one foot.

"I know what you want, you old troublemaker," the ostler murmured and the stallion nickered. "Lucky for you, there is a good store of apples and I am sufficiently glad to see you again that I will find you a few."

The Hawk looked up at Malcolm. "Will you be lingering, my lord?"

"Aye, I will stay the night, with your indulgence, and give the horses a rest before riding home again."

"So soon?" the Hawk asked as Malcolm dismounted. "You know you are welcome to stay."

Malcolm smiled. "I would be glad to spend time at Inverfyre, and hear all your tidings." He shook hands with his uncle. "But Catriona is with child."

"You should have brought her."

"She does not yet have a confidence in the saddle for long journeys, and she has been unwell with this pregnancy. I do not wish to leave her alone for long, but I had to see this horse restored to his rightful place." Malcolm nodded to his companion who dismounted and helped the ostler to lead the horses to the stable.

"There has been a cut on Tyr's flank that was not quickly tended," the Hawk noted with a frown as they watched the horses depart. "It mars his coat."

"But not his gait," Malcolm said. "It was only a nick, sufficient to startle him."

"From the assault upon Quentin," Mhairi said. "The thieves compelled the horse to bolt."

Malcolm looked between them. "Then this horse *was* given to one of your men? I knew only that Tyr had been sent to Inverfyre."

"Tyr was a gift to my Captain of the Guard, many years ago," the Hawk said. "To commemorate his loyal service. I am glad to see that the steed is healthy and returned."

115

"Then you will keep him here?"

"Of course. Thank you." The Hawk eyed his nephew. "How did you find Tyr?"

"I did not. It was my comrade Rafael. He was much impressed by the steeds of Ravensmuir when he visited Scotland. When he spied Tyr for sale, he guessed his ancestry immediately and bought him just to send him home." Malcolm's smile was rueful. "I owe Rafael good coin for this favor."

"And Elizabeth will ensure that you pay your due," the Hawk teased, referring to Malcolm's sister who had married Rafael. "How does she fare?"

"Well enough, I would wager. They have two sons already and his man brought a missive that shares the news that she is with child again."

"Good," the Hawk said. "I am glad that she is happy."

Malcolm frowned. "But I do not understand. How did Tyr come to be in Spain?"

"Papa cast Quentin out seven years ago," Mhairi supplied, even as her father's lips thinned. "He rode south to find work as a mercenary and was robbed in Spain."

Malcolm's frown deepened. "There are treacherous regions, to be sure, and often they are in the vicinities where mercenaries can find labor. A stallion like this would draw a covetous eye. But this knight must have survived for you to know his misfortune."

"Aye, he returned to Inverfyre a few weeks ago and aided in the killing of the MacLarens," the

Hawk contributed.

"For which Papa sent him away again," Mhairi said, not troubling to hide her bitterness. "Instead of offering a sanctuary to a knight who had served him well, he dispatched him from Inverfyre again."

"He did not need pity, Mhairi," the Hawk said. "He had need of labor."

Malcolm looked between father and daughter, his expression considering. "What was the crime of this Quentin, that he should have been dispatched in the first place?"

"Have you not guessed that it involved my daughter?" the Hawk asked. His expression was stony and his tone grim as he continued. "He taught Mhairi the arts of war, when she was but eleven summers of age, and continued to do so in defiance of my express command that he cease."

"I wanted to know," Mhairi said. "I entreated him to teach me. Your argument, Papa, is with me, not with Quentin."

The Hawk's voice softened. "I have no argument with you, Mhairi. Your nature is as it is, and I would not change it."

"But..."

"Indeed, you remind me forcibly of your mother, who also will not readily surrender a notion once she has a grip upon it."

"Because you are wrong!"

The Hawk raised his voice slightly. "I am not. I would ensure your happiness."

"I will not have any, not with Quentin gone

forever."

"And where is it writ that he is gone forever?" The Hawk clicked his tongue. "You and your mother are quick to condemn me, but I know you and your nature, daughter mine. Trust me to see to your best interests."

Mhairi set her lips, just as convinced of her view as ever, but her father gave no indication that she had swayed his thinking at all.

"Praise be that I have no daughters," Malcolm said, half under his breath.

"Yet," the Hawk replied, biting off the word. "I assure you that they will prompt an abundance of grey hair if you do have any." He clapped Malcolm on the shoulder. "Come to the hall and take refreshment. The ostler will send your man to us once the horses are settled and I would hear the tidings from Ravensmuir and Kinfairlie."

"You would hear how Gawain and Avery fare with their training," Malcolm teased.

"And you cannot blame a father for that," the Hawk replied easily. He gave Mhairi a steady look, but she did not change her defiant posture.

Nor did she follow the pair.

Her father did not think Quentin was worthy of her. She could see the truth of it. And it vexed her mightily that there was little she could do to change his mind. She had given her promise to her father and she would keep it, but she wished she knew his scheme. Where had he sent Quentin?

Would Quentin return to Inverfyre? She had

doubted it, but now thought of the stallion. Her father had welcomed Tyr's return and said the horse could remain.

Perhaps he only meant to give the destrier to someone else. It was a disappointing notion, but Mhairi had no opportunity to dwell upon it.

For there was another arrival at the gates.

A knight with two squires.

They rode with haste, their steeds galloping up the road, the knight in the lead. He tugged off his helmet when he approached the gates and his hair shone auburn in the sunlight.

Mhairi raised her hands to her lips and gasped aloud.

She heard her father chuckle, and suggest to Malcolm that they wait.

Then Quentin swept through the village, coming to a halt before her father. He cast her a sparkling glance, then dismounted with grace. He strode to her father and dropped to one knee, presenting a missive to the Hawk.

"Laird Garrett sends his good wishes to you and yours for the Yule, my lord, and also his thanks."

The Hawk smiled. "Aye?" He gestured and Quentin stood again.

"Aye. And I would thank you, too, sir, for the recommendation. I am now Captain of the Guard at Killairig, and as such, I am in need of a wife. I would humbly request the honor of your daughter's hand in mine."

Mhairi gasped in delight.

Her father smiled. "And I would be honored to grant it to you, provided the lady herself agrees." He turned to her, inviting her to join them with a gesture, and Mhairi laughed as she ran to Quentin's side.

"Of course!" she said, knowing her pleasure showed.

Quentin took her hand in his and bent over it, touching his lips to her fingers. "We will have many challenges before us, Mhairi. Killairig is not so rich as Inverfyre. It has been destroyed and recently rebuilt..."

"And we shall be a part of making it better than it was before," she concluded with enthusiasm. "I do not care where we are, Quentin, so long as I am with you."

"And so long as I have my valiant warrior maiden by my side, I know we will triumph," Quentin concluded. He drew her closer and smiled down at her, his fingertip touching her cheek. "Be mine," he murmured for her ears alone and Mhairi nodded agreement.

"Only yours," she agreed and saw the flicker of pleasure in his gaze.

"Forever allied," he murmured, then bent to capture her lips beneath his own once more. Heat surged through Mhairi, heat and satisfaction, and happiness for their shared future. She cast her arms around Quentin's neck and let him lift her to her toes as she returned his kiss with abandon. The people of Inverfyre cheered their approval.

"The honeysuckle and the hazel," her father said when they finally parted. Mhairi saw that her mother, sister and brother had joined the party in the bailey.

"United forever," her mother concluded. "As they should be."

The Hawk gestured to the prancing destrier that had just returned with Malcolm. "And it appears that a wedding gift has arrived in a most timely manner."

"Tyr!" Quentin cried with heartfelt delight and Mhairi smiled as he greeted the steed. He held her hand fast in his own and turned to her, his pleasure more than clear. "And so it is that my pupil has made my dreams come true," he murmured as he drew her close again. "I love you, Mhairi, and I vow to spend my days and nights ensuring that your every dream comes true."

"It already has," she confided in him, raising her lips for his kiss. They would dance on the Yule together to celebrate their nuptials, dance as they had in her dream, and it would be only the beginning of their adventure together.

Mhairi could scarce wait to begin.

The story of the siblings at Inverfyre continues with

THE RUNAWAY BRIDE
The Brides of Inverfyre #2

Coming in October 2018!

The Brides of Inverfyre series continues the tale of the
family at Ravensmuir and Kinfairlie.

Begin the series with
THE ROGUE,
book #1 of the *Rogues of Ravensmuir*,
or with
THE BEAUTY BRIDE,
book #1 of the *Jewels of Kinfairlie*.

The Hawk and Aileen's story is
THE WARRIOR,
book #3 of the *Rogues of Ravensmuir*.

Learn more about the world of Ravensmuir,
Kinfairlie and Inverfyre
—and download free family trees—
on Claire's website:

HTTP://DELACROIX.NET

ABOUT THE AUTHOR

Deborah Cooke sold her first book in 1992, a medieval romance called published under her pseudonym Claire Delacroix. Since then, she has published over fifty novels in a wide variety of sub-genres, including historical romance, contemporary romance, and paranormal romance. She has published under the names Claire Delacroix, Claire Cross and Deborah Cooke. **The Beauty**, part of her successful Bride Quest series of historical romances, was her first title to land on the *New York Times* List of Bestselling Books. Her books routinely appear on other bestseller lists and have won numerous awards. In 2009, she was the writer-in-residence at the Toronto Public Library, the first time the library has hosted a residency focused on the romance genre. In 2012, she was honored to receive the Romance Writers of America's Mentor of the Year Award.

Currently, she writes historical romances as Claire Delacroix. She also writes paranormal romances and contemporary romances under the name Deborah Cooke. Deborah lives in Canada with her husband and family, as well as far too many unfinished knitting projects.

To learn more about her books, visit her websites:
http://delacroix.net
http://deborahcooke.com